THE
FOOTBALL
REBELS

THE FOOTBALL REBELS

— Jackson Scholz —

A Beech Tree Paperback Book
New York

Copyright © 1960 by Jackson Scholz.
Reissued by both Morrow Junior Books and Beech Tree Books in 1993 with
changes that update the text for contemporary readers.

All rights reserved. No part of this book may be reproduced or utilized in any
form or by any means, electronic or mechanical, including photocopying,
recording, or by any information storage and retrieval system, without
permission in writing from the Publisher. Inquiries should be addressed to
William Morrow and Company, Inc., 1350 Avenue of the Americas, New York,
NY 10019.
Book Design by Logo Studios/B. Gold.
Printed in the United States of America.

10 9 8 7 6 5 4 3 2 1

Library of Congress Cataloging-in-Publication Data
Scholz, Jackson Volney.
The football rebels / Jackson Scholz.   p.   cm.
Summary: Unable to make the varsity football team at Midwestern
University, freshman Clint Martin decides to buck the athletic
organization by starting his own informal team made up of any
students who want to play football.
ISBN 0-688-12643-X
[1. Football—Fiction.   2. Universities and colleges—Fiction.]
I. Title. PZ7.S37Fo 1993 [Fic]—dc20 92-43376 CIP AC

PUBLISHER'S NOTE

Football is played much differently today than it was in the 1960's. There have been alterations in equipment and safety standards, but the most significant changes have resulted from new substitution rules. Traditional substitution rules reflected football's origins in rugby and stated that a player who left the game in one quarter could not return until the following quarter. This led most team members to play on both offense and defense; many would play an entire game without once leaving the field. These early players were therefore skilled at many positions, and a star player, like Clint Martin in *The Football Rebels,* might have been the first-string quarterback, safety, punter, placekicker, and kick returner. The incredible conditioning required to play sixty continuous minutes of football on both sides of the line of scrimmage earned these players the nickname "ironmen."

Fielding a team of eleven "ironmen" demanded an offense constructed around their basic all-around abilities. Early football teams used a simple offensive strategy—running the ball almost exclusively and passing only when necessary. For the power and versatility this strategy required, there was no better offensive weapon than the T-formation. In this configuration, the quarterback lined up directly behind the center, with the fullback several yards behind him. Two halfbacks flanked the fullback, forming a "T" in the backfield. The left and right ends were positioned on the line and, although eligible for pass receptions, were used primarily as blockers. By placing this many players close to the ball, the "T" enabled teams to block powerfully and produce consistent running gains. On a given play, the quarterback could hand the ball off to any of his three runningbacks, run with it himself, or throw a pass to one of the two ends for a quick completion. This play-calling flexibility kept defenses guessing while still providing the offensive punch necessary to win football games.

Soon after World War II, professional football changed its rules to allow unlimited substitutions. This policy was instituted to accommodate the sudden flood of talented young war veterans who were now eager to make their mark on the professional gridiron. As coaches became accustomed to these new substitution rules, they realized that they could develop specialty players who were excellent at just one position rather than moderately skilled in several. Defensive coordinators sought huge but slow defensive linemen to stop the T-formation offense in its tracks. Offensive coordinators responded with light, fast receivers and quarterbacks with powerful arms to get the ball to them. Touchdowns could be scored quickly and consistently, and coaches scrambled to accommodate this new passing attack. The slow moving, tightly packed T-formation was soon made obsolete by intricate pass-oriented formations with more eligible receivers on the line and fewer runningbacks in the backfield. Catching the fever of this exciting brand of football, college and semi-professional leagues followed suit and changed their substitution rules in the mid-1960's.

Nowadays, the only place to see the T-formation is in high school and college football, where the teams have neither the practice time nor the skilled players to develop complex offensive schemes. The simplicity and power of the T-formation and its modern variation, the wishbone, still give these games the grinding "fourth-down-and-inches-to-go" excitement of old-time football that Jackson Scholz has captured and immortalized in his football novels *Rookie Quarterback* and *The Football Rebels*.

THE FOOTBALL REBELS

CHAPTER
1

When people spoke of football in connection with Midwestern University they spoke of it, not always with approval, with the awe reserved for some strange hungry monster. Clint Martin was aware of this. It cannot be said that he reported for the freshman squad wide-eyed and innocent, because he knew the cards were stacked against him from the start.

The men who ruled Midwestern's formidable squad, the Vulcans, would not be interested in kids like Clint—inexperienced boys with undistinguished high-school records. Midwestern shopped for its gridiron material, combining the country for hot prospects before sending out recruiting teams, seasoned experts who seldom let a young fish off the hook.

These men, in the course of business, expected to

encounter equally seasoned experts from other football colleges, and were prepared for these encounters with a huge supply of guile, unlimited gall, and the spell-binding technique of a criminal lawyer. The law of the recruiting jungle was quite simple—get your man. Offer all the inducements permitted by the intercollegiate rules, and don't come back without him. None of these experts, needless to say, had cast a lure at Clint.

Going out for football was his own idea, a futile idea maybe, but one he could not shake. His confidence was meager, sustained only by a stubbornness which kept him moving in the direction of the Athletic Center, an elaborate modern layout dedicated to football and maintained by football revenue.

Clint Martin did not look like good football material. He had the height, six feet, but not the weight; he tipped the scales at 160 pounds. He was an angular young man, whose big-boned frame left room for a good deal more flesh. He walked with a loose stride which suggested a coltish lack of maturity and coordination.

His face, however, was surprisingly mature for a college freshman. The lines were strong and promised to be permanent. The angle of his jaw and the set of his lips showed stubbornness, but his gray-blue eyes with tiny crow's-feet at the corners, gave the impression that, though stubborn, he was not bullheaded, and could mix determination with discretion.

He hoped the needed extra weight would come in time. He was resentful because he had to wait for it, and because he lacked the patience waiting would require. Most of all, at the moment, he resented the driving urge within him to play football, for he believed the situation was hopeless. He almost wished he had chosen a smaller college, where he might have had a chance to play the game, instead of choosing Midwestern, as he had done, for its excellent curriculum in metallurgy, one of the finest in the country.

His pace faltered as he approached the imposing layout of the Athletic Center, built on three sides of a rectangle. The buildings were made of white, rough stone. The Administration Building, at the far end of the rectangle, was devoted entirely to the complicated process of running a big-business athletic institution. It contained the executive offices as well as the offices of coaches and assistant coaches.

The huge bulk of the gymnasium loomed on the left. The immense field house with its graceful cantilever roof was on the right. It contained a cinder running track constructed around an abbreviated football field to be used in rainy weather. It could seat eight thousand fans for basketball games and indoor track meets.

In the space bounded by the three sides, there was a small park containing trees, a fountain in the center, and stone benches for the weary. It formed the approach to the Administration Building, and Clint, walking through such grandeur, was completely and frankly awed.

Inside the building, Clint encountered nothing but efficiency. Signs with pointing arrows faced him. One read: *Candidates with Athletic Scholarships.* The one applying to Clint announced in much smaller letters: *Candidates without Athletic Scholarships.* The arrows on the signs pointed in opposite directions.

Clint had started in the direction indicated, when he heard footsteps behind him. A voice at his shoulder said, "Are you about to stick your neck out too?"

Clint turned and faced a man of approximately his own age and height. The other, however, was considerably heavier, but this did not detract from his ease of movement. He had a wide, engaging mouth, and lively amber eyes which seemed to challenge life to keep him well amused. Clint liked his looks.

"Why, yes," said Clint. "I thought I'd take a whirl at it just to see how long I can hang on."

"Me too. I probably need my head examined, but I'm afraid to take the chance. They might find nothing in there but sawdust. I'm Yancy Tolliver."

"Clint Martin."

"I'm sure glad to find another student."

Clint nodded, understanding Yancy's use of the term. A "student," in the athletic jargon of Midwestern, was a young chump who was stupid enough to report for football without the benefit of an athletic scholarship.

They reached their destination at the end of a long corridor. A half dozen other students, waiting their turn, were leaning against the wall in various stages of impatience and annoyance. The office door was open. The sound of voices and a typewriter could be heard. The men entered one by one and came out with their dispositions unimproved. When the man ahead of Clint went in, Clint was close enough to the door to distinguish words. His temper, reliable for the most part, began to rise.

A bored voice said, "O.K., Bud, what's your name?"

Other questions followed, the typewriter clattering down the answers.

"Where'd you play football?"

"I've never played."

"What?" There was outrage in the tone.

"You heard me."

There was an unpleasant burst of laughter. "Bud, you slay me. Maybe you've got nothing to do but waste my time and your own." There was a brief silence.

Then the voice said, "Oh, well, I guess it's your funeral. This card'll get you a uniform. See you in the morgue. Next!"

A husky kid came out, hot-eyed. "Close," he muttered. "Mighty close. I almost let him have it in the teeth."

Clint entered the office in an uncertain frame of mind. He had not liked what he had heard, and now he did not care for what he saw.

The man behind the typewriter was obviously a student in the accepted sense of the word. He was a small man, a fact which probably accounted for his attitude of superiority toward larger men. He had a big pipe in his teeth, believing, probably, that it added to his manliness. He was obviously still amused at the way he had dusted off the previous candidate.

As Clint stood waiting beside the desk, the little man behind the typewriter very deliberately lit his pipe and then blew the smoke at Clint. "O.K., Bud," he said. "What's your name?"

Blinking against the smoke, Clint rested both hands on the desk, bringing him considerably closer to the man behind it. "Listen, Buster," he said in a flat voice. "Let's get something straightened out before you go into your dance."

After a startled glance, the little man bristled. "There's nothing to get straightened out," he snapped.

"I'm here to ask the questions and you're here to answer them. Now what's your name?"

"I'm afraid you're not getting the idea," Clint told him, with deceptive patience. "I'm here to sign up for freshman football, not to be shoved around by a little jerk like you."

The clerk came half out of his chair, then wisely changed his mind. "You can't talk to me like that!" he spluttered.

"Why not?" Clint asked him reasonably. "What have I got to lose? I probably won't last long as a football player, so what's to keep me from shoving that pipe down your throat while I happen to be in the mood?"

The clerk considered this with noticeable loss of color. He hastily removed his pipe and laid it on the desk.

"You're learning," Clint approved. "Now go ahead and ask the questions without any of your cute side remarks."

The interview was brief and businesslike, though surly. There was no derogatory comment when Clint revealed his past football experience as a second-string high school quarterback.

When Clint left the office, Yancy, grinning, met him in the doorway. "Well now," said Yancy, staring at the man behind the desk, "So *that's* the bunny rabbit who was making all those loud noises. And you," he said reprovingly to Clint, "didn't leave me anything to chew on. Stick around. I'll be right out."

When they left the building, Clint was thoughtful and slightly gloomy.

"Cheer up," Yancy said. "You've done your good deed for the day. That little squirt'll behave himself from now on."

"Yeah, he'll mind his manners."

"And so?"

"Well," Clint answered slowly, "it's just that the whole thing goes far beyond the little guy in the office. He's unimportant—a small cog in a big machine. But when a weevil like that is permitted to treat us the way he did, it's pretty obvious we don't amount to much and will amount to even less when we climb into a football suit."

"So what do we do now—tear up these little cards that'll get us an outfit?"

"If we had any brains we probably would," said Clint. "My trouble is, I hate to quit when I've started something."

"I wouldn't exactly consider that a weakness," Yancy said. "I've got a little of it in me too. So tomorrow we report for football—heaven help us."

Considering the matter settled, Clint asked, "Where are you living?"

"Radfield Dormitory, second floor."

"Me too," said Clint, with pleasure.

Both Clint and Yancy decided to go back to the dormitory. When they reached it, Clint said, "We may not like the football setup here, but we certainly can't squawk about having a place like this to live in."

The three-story building, also built with white stone, contained a spacious lobby, comparable to that of a fine hotel. There was a large restaurant opposite the lobby, where excellent meals were included in the rental of the rooms. Two self-service elevators made it easy to reach the upper floors.

The rooms were reasonably large, well-lit and well-furnished, and the students had the choice of single or double rooms. Clint had chosen to live by himself, knowing that he could do a better job of studying without the distraction of a roommate. He felt he could be happy here unless some outside factor—football, for instance—disturbed his contentment.

CHAPTER
2

Clint and Yancy left the dormitory together on the following afternoon, heading with similar misgivings toward the Athletic Center. The equipment room, they learned, was on the lower floor of the gymnasium. The room was long and narrow. A broad counter extended in front of many bins containing uniforms, pads, shoes, and helmets.

The bins nearest to the entrance contained expensive new equipment, and Clint was not surprised when, after a glance at the color of the proffered cards, the counter man sent him and Yancy to the far end of the room. Here, another counter man, after a quick guess at their size, tossed them a bundle. Farther down, each was permitted to mention his shoe size before receiving football shoes.

As they left the room Yancy grumbled, "I feel like I've just been given an older brother's hand-me-downs."

"And you'll look like it too, when you get into those duds," Clint promised.

The dressing room accommodations for the students were less than elaborate. They were directed to a large locker room whose door sign read: *Freshman Football.* There were, however, no lockers available for students. Their lockers were a line of chairs along the wall.

"Oh, look!" said Yancy with sardonic pleasure. "We've even got a hook all to ourselves, right here on the wall."

"They think of everything," said Clint. "Do you suppose they'll let us take a shower when we come in?"

"A shower!" repeated Yancy, shocked. "Of course not. There's a hose outside for us to squirt on each other."

When each man untied the bundle containing his uniform, pads, and helmet, he found a sorry mess—old hand-me-downs bordering on raggedness.

Clint examined the splayed cleats of his sweat-stiffened shoes. "The last one to wear these," he told Yancy with conviction, "was a kangaroo."

There were other students in the group. Some accepted the situation stoically, others tried to reconcile themselves to this early evidence of their unimportance, and still others were vocally rebellious. When they drifted toward the field they were a ratty-looking bunch.

Clint had to laugh as he looked Yancy over. "Don't run too fast," he warned him, "or you'll run yourself right out of those pants."

"Stylish, aren't they?" agreed Yancy. "And that shirt of yours is nifty too. You could stuff a couple of footballs under it and nobody would know you had 'em."

The students were herded to one end of the broad practice area outside the stadium. They stood aimlessly around for half an hour or so before an assistant coach approached them, obviously resentful of the menial job assigned to him.

"My name's Blake," he told them gruffly.

He spaced them out and started them on calisthenics. After explaining what he wanted them to do, he relaxed as he counted out the cadence, letting the football men do all the work. He kept on counting while the students sweated, grunted, and began to lose their steam. When an occasional man slowed down through sheer exhaustion he was promptly singled out.

"You there!" Blake would bellow. "We don't want any goof-off artists around here! Show a little life or get off the field!"

He finally let them rest. The squad of fifty or so weary men flopped to the ground, trying to regain their breath. Blake, thumbs hooked in his belt, then made a speech.

"I'm being rough on you men," he admitted. "And it's only fair to warn you, I'll get rougher. You'll probably begin to hate my guts. Frankly I hope you don't, because that's not the way I want it. You've got to understand, however, that I've got a job to do. If there's any varsity material here, I've got to find it. Our time is badly limited, so it's got to be a rush job. I repeat— it'll be rough. It all boils down to a very simple thing— the survival of the fittest. I'm sorry it has to be that way, but you might as well know it from the start. Anyone can check out any time he wants to. It won't be held against him."

A voice from the squad called, "You're talking to *me*, mister. Slave drivers are out of date."

One of the men got up and began his wobbly progress toward the gym. Another wordlessly followed his example. Seven of them silently accepted the coach's invitation toward a less strenuous college life.

The workout continued, just as rough as Blake had promised. When Clint and Yancy finally started for the gym, they moved on dragging legs, too tired to talk.

The practice session on the following day was as

rugged as the first. Blake turned on the heat and kept it sizzling. Five more students left the squad.

Clint was completely bushed as he made his way back toward the gym. The elite freshman squad, in spruce new uniforms, was arriving at the same time. There was a slight jam-up at the door of the locker room, but Clint, plodding wearily on, was scarcely aware of what was happening.

As he entered the doorway, the misshapen cleats and the weariness of his legs threw him off balance, and he staggered toward a freshman player who was entering the door just as he was. In trying to regain balance Clint accidentally stepped on the other man's foot. He muttered, "Sorry," entirely unprepared for the violent shove which banged him against the opposite side of the door.

"Watch where you're going, you clumsy clown!" the man snarled.

Clint's legs almost buckled. He controlled them, staring more in surprise than anger at the man whose foot he had stepped on. Clint did not care for what he saw. The guy was big and broad-shouldered, outweighing Clint by some twenty pounds. He was handsome in a way that breeds distrust in other men. His hair was blond and curly. His pale eyes had a glassy sort of sheen.

Clint disliked him promptly, but he was too weary

in mind and body for his simmering anger to take hold. "I told you I was sorry," he said. "I didn't mean to step on you."

One of the other man's teammates, sensing trouble, said, "Take it easy, Bronco."

Bronco ignored the advice. When Clint started to move ahead, he stepped in front of him. "You students," Bronco said, "may be good for a big laugh, but we don't like to have you walking on us."

"It was an accident," said Clint, wanting nothing more than to sit down and rest.

"I say you did it on purpose."

"Then you're a liar."

Bronco's open hand caught Clint across the mouth. Clint scarcely knew what happened after that. He was never able to recall the moment clearly. He only knew in a vague way that the frustration of the football workout, his dislike of Bronco, and his outrage, at this instant, all managed to combine to create a huge explosion.

His first clear thought revealed to him that his fist had connected with something solid. His vision brought him the amazing sight of Bronco, out cold, being supported by the teammates who had caught him before he hit the floor. Amazement was upon their faces too. Clint started for the student section of the room.

Yancy followed him, repeating happily, "Oh lovely, lovely, lovely!"

Clint felt a hand on his elbow. He turned, found another freshman, then went tense in anticipation of more trouble. But there was no need for it. The man was grinning.

The freshman said, "We want to thank you."

Clint eyed the man, still wary.

The freshman went on, "That was Bronco Slade you knocked out. He's the fair-haired boy of the squad, the big first-money prize of the recruiting system, and he never lets anyone forget it. He's a slob. None of *us* can clobber him without getting bounced off the squad, so you're our boy. Please don't get the idea that any of the rest of us are like him."

"Well . . . thanks," said Clint, still confused.

When the freshman returned to his own group, Clint and Yancy relaxed on their chairs, gathering energy to take a bath.

"And where," demanded Yancy, "did you learn to throw a punch like that?"

"Darned if I know where it came from," Clint admitted honestly. "I've had a few brawls in my time, but I never uncorked one like that before. It'll be nice to remember that one, even if I never find another like it."

* * *

The daily student workouts continued at a pace which finally ground the squad down to thirty stubborn men who wouldn't quit. Clint's body became rawhide-tough. He even found, to his surprise, that he had gained a little weight. Both he and Yancy felt a certain pride that they could now withstand the punishment.

Coach Blake began to push himself as hard as he pushed any of the men, a wordless admission that he admired their guts. Attempting the futile job of being everywhere at once, he nevertheless began to get a few results. He seemed sincere in teaching them the things he knew, despite the terrific handicap of trying to teach inexperienced men, in so short a time, the complicated details of their jobs. No one man was capable of such a task.

Clint soaked up knowledge and experience like a thirsty sponge, and retained most of it. He was eager to learn more and more about the game of football, but wise enough to know that he had barely scratched the surface of the many things a quarterback must know. He was astonished, nevertheless, at the improvement in his game as compared with the brand of football he had played in high school.

Yancy expressed the same thought. "If I'd been as good an end as this in high school," he said soberly, "I might have been recruited."

Clint's chief handicap, at this stage, was entirely

physical, a condition he could not control. His brain told him to do certain things which his muscles seemed incapable of doing properly. This built up a helpless anger in him which he usually managed to subdue by reason, telling himself that his physical maturity was slow in coming, though definitely on the way. On these occasions he consoled himself with the knowledge that he was doing the thing he loved most—playing football. He stubbornly refused to face the fact that his football-playing days would soon be over. His only acknowledgment of this was the panicky effort he was making to cram as much football as possible into the brief remaining time.

Concern for his own problems did not prevent his analyzing the general progress of the squad. It was not encouraging. There was, undoubtedly, a lot of good football material on the squad—men who might conceivably make the varsity, with considerably more training and personal attention, but there was no chance of their getting this. There was only one man, Dutch Schwartz, a speedy 230-pound lineman, who was almost certain to be recognized and promoted to the freshman squad.

Most of the players could hope to play in only one game, the game the athletic department dangled before the students' eyes, as a reward. It was called the "graduation exercises," a sardonic term applied to the event which was designated to terminate their brief career in college football. The students would be allowed to play an exhibition game against the freshmen.

The outcome of the game would never be in doubt, and the athletic bigwigs of Midwestern would have proved their point. It would be demonstrated that the coaches were not entirely blind to unrecruited talent, and the superiority of the freshmen would justify their recruiting system. The game would, in its way, be a parting pat on the back for the students, a farewell, which, in effect, said, "Sorry, boys, you had your chance and just weren't good enough. We didn't think you would be."

"What puzzles me," said Yancy, a few days before the game, "is why the guys are getting all steamed up about it. They all know what's going to happen to them, yet they keep on working as if they had a chance to win."

"You're working like that too," Clint pointed out.

"Huh?" said Yancy, startled, as if the thought was new to him. "Why, yeah, I guess I am."

"Why?"

"I'm not too sure."

"Have you given up all hope that you might show enough stuff in the game to catch the eye of the Varsity coaches?"

Yancy's guilty look betrayed him. He said sheepishly, "Well . . . maybe I might figure it that way."

"You know perfectly well you do," said Clint. "I'm ashamed to admit it, but so do I. So does every man on the squad."

Yancy grinned and said, "We could be right at that."

"Well, at least we'll be ready for a fight," Clint prophesied.

CHAPTER
3

When the day of the freshman game arrived, Clint's prophecy proved accurate. The students were drawn to a fine edge as they climbed into their shabby uniforms. They were winding themselves up for their last big effort, their final chance at football recognition.

By contrast, the freshman squad across the room was relaxed and confident, as they had a right to be. As far as the freshmen were concerned, the game was just another workout. The horseplay and kidding were routine. Today, however, they were not confined entirely to the squad.

Bronco Slade was the offender. He called out to the students, "Hey, you guys! Have you got your life insurance all paid up?"

None of the students thought it funny and few of the freshmen gave the clumsy gag a tumble.

Bronco tried again. "It's not too late to quit," he called. "You guys would be smart to walk out of here while you've still got the chance. We don't want any injured students on our conscience."

Clint heard warning rumbles from the men near him. "Save it for the game," he quickly advised them.

An echo came from the freshman side. "O.K.," said a voice. "Knock it off!"

Bronco whirled to put up an argument, but changed his mind when he saw the size of the lineman who had spoken. A further check was clamped on Bronco's ideas of humor by the warning looks on the faces of his teammates. He shrugged elaborately and went about his business.

The students were hot-eyed and fuming as they left the gym. Clint had a feeling that Bronco Slade might have aided the student cause considerably—that these guys, in their present frame of mind, might hand the freshmen a surprise.

Coach Blake, noting the temper of the squad, nodded brief approval. He sent them through a warm-up, then gathered them about him just before the game was called. "I'm not feeding you men any hogwash to make you think you have a chance to lick these guys," he said. "I think, however, you can hand them quite a jolt. Just do your best, and whatever happens I'll be proud of you."

Clint, as quarterback and acting captain of the squad, went to the center of the field for the coin-tossing ceremony. It was a practice field, of course. The stadium could not be used for such an unimportant game as this. There was no seating arrangement for the spectators. There was no need, because the fans were few and anything but excited. They scattered themselves around the side lines with the air of people who had nothing better to do.

Clint won the toss. On previous instructions from the coach he elected to receive. His men stationed themselves at their end of the field, while Bronco Slade teed up the ball. A speedy student by the name of Archer had the honor spot in front of the goal posts. Clint, on the right, was guilty of hoping that the ball would not come to him. His nerves were quivering and his legs felt weak. The referee's whistle sounded. Bronco, making the short run, drove his toe into the ball.

It was a good kick, high and deep. Its direction, though, was not what Clint would have chosen. With a snort of alarm he watched it come directly at him. He tried to remember what he had learned, to reach for the ball, take the first impact with his hands, palms up, then ease it back into his body. Above all, *watch* the ball—watch it every instant.

Something got fouled up. His timing must have been a little off. He may have been too aware of the thundering feet bearing down upon him. His hands, at any rate, failed to form the proper cushion. The ball banged too hard against his chest. With a gasp of horror he watched it bound a few feet into the air. Then he made a frantic lunge and, by some miracle, retrieved it.

When he started running in his slightly awkward way, the scene in front of him was not encouraging. The freshmen were converging on him like a platoon of speedy tanks. His teammates did their best to make a path, but overeagerness and inexperience were poor weapons. The freshmen swept aside the students as if they were sweeping leaves. Two men hit Clint before he was buried beneath an avalanche of freshmen.

He was far from sure that he could move, even when the men unpiled. He tried his legs first, and they responded. Then he found that his arms would still work. Aside from a moderate loss of breath he found himself still intact, a source of considerable satisfaction. It proved, for what it was worth, that he could take it. The rugged training under Blake was paying off.

It was time for the first wave of discouragement yet to Clint's surprise it did not come. The strong stimulus of action came instead, and oddly enough, confidence came too. He was grinning when he met the apologetic eyes of his teammates. Their aspect

changed as some of Clint's assurance was com-
municated to them.

Clint had been pulled down on the thirteen-yard
line, and as the students came into the huddle, it was
time for him to call the first signal of the game. His
choice was restricted. Blake, of necessity, had been
forced to keep the students' plays as simple and un-
complicated as he could. There had been no time to
teach them tricky stuff, and even the rudimentary
plays they had been able to absorb had not been
learned too well.

Clint shot a quick look at the freshmen—not that
he expected to learn much from what he saw. They
were definitely free from any worries, though serious
enough, for the most part. The exception was Bronco
Slade, who stood, arms folded, in the left linebacker
spot, obviously contemptuous and amused.

Clint noticed that the freshman defense was
drawn in fairly tight, in the reasonable assumption that
the students would not try anything foolish in the
shadow of their own goal posts. Clint, however,
thought it was a poor assumption. In this game the
students had nothing to lose by taking chances, and
the only weapon they possessed was a feeble one—
merely the element of surprise.

Clint's call for a first-down pass brought grunts of
approval from the huddle. The students came up to the

line fast in a tight formation. Clint moved behind the center, checked the positions of his split-T, then felt the ball slap solidly into his hands. He whirled and faked a handoff to his fullback who, in turn, faked a buck off tackle.

The deception, though mediocre, was as good as Clint could hope for. The freshmen, less alert than they should have been, fell for it. Instead of crashing through the line to mess things up in the student back-field, the freshmen funneled in to stop the line plunge, leaving Clint more time than he deserved to fade back for the pass.

Yancy, his right end, cut toward the side line and was in the open. Clint drew a bead on a point ahead of Yancy and let fly. It was a good pass, probably a lucky one for a man with Clint's brief training. The ball, it is true, wobbled a little in the air, but it was pretty well on the beam. Yancy hauled it in after a long stretch and set sail for pay dirt.

Yancy had good speed but nothing to match that of the freshman playing in the deep defensive spot. The kid could run like a whippet. He overhauled Yancy on the freshman thirty-two-yard line and banged him out-of-bounds. It was, nevertheless, a spectacular gain, and a severe jolt to the freshmen. They were poised and ready this time as they came to the line of scrimmage.

Clint, playing a long hunch, called the same play

for the second time, hoping the freshmen would not think him stupid enough to force his luck that far. The hunch was sound, but the execution of the play was anything but easy. The freshman line did not pick any daisies. They clawed their way into the student back-field, intending to stop the play before it got under way.

Clint had less time to fade and pick his target. He ducked the high grab of a big lineman, managing to regain some sort of balance before he made his throw. It was hurried, merely aimed as hard as he could throw it at some vague spot where he hoped he might find Yancy—which, by a freak of chance, he did.

It was one of those things like a hole in one in golf. Yancy reached out, grabbed the ball, and almost stumbled in his surprise. He headed for the end zone, reaching the four-yard line before the freshman safety smacked him out-of-bounds again.

The freshmen, still suffering from shock, were setups for the moment when Clint played his ace, Dutch Schwartz, assuming that none of the freshmen would expect a man of Dutch's caliber in the student line. Clint called a simple power play directly through Dutch Schwartz, with the fullback carrying the ball. The fresh-men would undoubtedly be expecting a line play in a situation such as this—a chance Clint had to take.

"Can you give us a hole, Dutch?" Clint asked in the huddle.

"You can drive a truck through it," Dutch promised.

He was almost right. He exploded like a bomb into the freshman line, splitting it wide open. The fullback, taking the handoff from Clint, was almost riding on the big man's back when Dutch carried him across the goal line.

Even though they missed the try for the extra point, the students were hopped up and slightly wacky over this proof of their ability. Clint hated to disillusion them, but he knew it was his job, because none of them were thinking clearly. "Come out of the clouds!" he told them sharply. "We were lucky, and you know it."

They nodded vaguely, still excited, quivering to get their hands upon the freshmen once more.

They had their chance. The freshmen ran back a poor kickoff to the midfield stripe, then set to work like some impersonal machine to prove what they were there to prove—that the student squad was nothing but a bunch of fumblers.

Bronco, calling the freshman signals, gave himself the breaks. He carried on the first two plays, found holes, and slashed his way to first-down gains. The guy was good. Clint grudgingly admitted it, if only to himself.

The students, on the other hand, were worse than they should have been. Overexcited and falsely confident, they behaved like chickens with a hawk above them, forgetting what they had been taught, in their wild scramble to prove that they were football players.

Clint called time out. "Open your parachutes and come back to earth," he told them. "You're going off half-cocked without giving yourself a chance to think what you're doing. You've worked yourselves into such a lather you've forgotten all you ever knew about football. We may be pretty bad, but we're not as bad as you're making us look. Shake your brains back where they belong and let's go to work."

Clint's rough advice brought angry grumbles. It also served the purpose he had hoped it might, focusing the students' attention on their immediate problems, rather than upon the shimmering fantasy that they might have a chance to lick the freshmen. Their eyes were saner and their movements smoother when the referee called time in.

The freshmen set another running play in motion, sweeping the right end following a fake line plunge. A couple of the student linebackers were sucked in, but not all of them. Two players remembered Clint's advice to try to solve the pattern of the play before committing themselves. This pair, together with Clint, ignored the line plunge and started to move wide with Bronco Slade as he tried to flank the student line.

Yancy played his end position with intelligence.

He refused to be boxed out of the opening through which Bronco had planned to swerve, thereby forcing Bronco to sweep wider than he had intended. This gave Clint and the other two defense men time to cut across in Bronco's path.

Clint yelled, "Get the blockers!"

His teammates did a sloppy but earnest job of tangling with the two men blocking out in front of Bronco, causing enough delay to make Bronco cut back from the side line toward the spot where Clint was waiting for him. Clint was able, fortunately, to catch Bronco in an instant of hesitation, which made the impact of the tackle considerably less than it might have been. Even so, Clint knew he had banged into a mighty solid chunk of meat. When the two men hit the ground together, Clint hoped nothing inside him had been shaken loose. It certainly felt as if it had.

"You lucky jerk!" rasped Bronco.

Clint let it pass. He got up, shook himself, and found everything in working order. He noted with satisfaction that Bronco had failed, this time, to make a first down—merely five yards. It was, of course, a healthy gain, but under the circumstances it appeared as if the students might be tightening their defense a little.

On the next play, Bronco sent his fullback on an experimental plunge over Dutch Schwartz's side of the line. The experiment was not successful. Dutch dug in, hunched his massive shoulders, and stopped the power play for a two-yard gain.

Bronco tried the other side of the line next time, packing the mail himself. He faked a sweep around the end, then cut back off-tackle, where the freshman forward wall had carved a huge inviting hole, neglecting nothing but a welcome mat. Bronco thundered through the hole, gaining speed with every stride.

Clint, partially fooled by the play, was a couple of strides out of position, in no spot to make the tackle. He was angry at himself as he scrambled back for a long-chance try to pull down Bronco, who could have easily avoided Clint for a long run, possibly a touchdown.

Bronco, however, had plans of his own, which obviously did not include a touchdown. Whatever disappointment Clint may have felt over missing the tackle was soon erased by Bronco. He swerved suddenly in mid-stride, placing Clint directly in his path. He came blasting in, knees pumping high. He smashed wickedly into Clint before Clint had time to set himself for the tackle.

They both went down. Clint got the worst of it, as Bronco had intended. Clint felt as if he had been hammered with a pair of baseball bats, but a surge of anger helped to offset the pain. He managed to be first on his feet and did not miss the look of shocked surprise in

Bronco's eyes. He glanced indifferently at Bronco before walking away, with the casual air of a man who made such tackles as a routine matter. It required an effort, but Clint pulled it off, believing, at the moment, that he could even have managed it with a pair of broken legs.

Bronco's run had carved out another first down, and nothing but a break of luck prevented the freshmen from going all the way. A bungled signal in the freshman backfield resulted in a fumble, recovered by Dutch Schwartz, who came plowing through the line. So the students had another chance on the offensive. It did not last long. Clint tried to get another pass away but had to eat the ball when he found his receivers covered like a tent. An avalanche of freshman linemen landed on him when he tried to run the ball himself. He lost six yards.

An end sweep, failing to get the proper blocking, fizzled out at the line of scrimmage. Clint placed the burden of the next play on Dutch Schwartz. Dutch handed them four yards, fourth down, twelve to go. Clint dropped back to kick. He was badly rushed. The ball squirted off the side of his foot, going out-of-bounds eight yards beyond the line of scrimmage.

The freshmen did not fumble this time. Two running plays gained eleven yards. Bronco went to the air then, for the first time in the game. He had all the time he needed, behind airtight protection. The students belatedly tried to cover the receivers. They might as well have tried to cover a flock of birds. Bronco's pass, a beauty, found a man wide open in the end zone. They kicked the extra point and went ahead, 7-6.

The freshmen kicked off again. The students did their best, but their best was far, far from enough. Whatever latent talent they possessed was cramped and smothered by inadequate coaching and woeful lack of experience. When the freshmen double-teamed efficiently on Dutch they robbed Clint of his one offensive and defensive threat.

Bronco, while carrying the ball, found the opportunity to run Clint down again, a maneuver which proved to be an error of judgment on Bronco's part. Clint survived the crash, but the freshman coach yanked Bronco from the game, probably reminding Bronco that he was in there to score touchdowns rather than engage in a personal feud.

The students hoped that Bronco's exit from the game might help their cause, but the hope was brief. The freshmen kept on rolling. The students, though they battled gamely, simply did not have the stuff, and matters went from bad to worse when they began to tire. They lacked reserves, while the freshman squad had plenty of good men on the bench. When the game became a farce, the coaches called it off, stopping the one-sided battle before the end of the first half.

As the battered and discouraged students left the field, Blake met them, his face sober. "I'm sorry, men," he said. No one could question his sincerity. "You did your best. You looked better than anyone expected. I'm proud of you."

He turned away abruptly. There was nothing more to say, nothing except to tell these courageous youngsters that their football career at Midwestern was ended.

CHAPTER
4

Clint and Yancy were relaxing in Clint's room some hours later, trying to ease their aching bones and muscles into less painful positions. It was hard to do. An occasional grunt or groan bore testimony to their aches and pains. A cloud of gloom hung heavy in the room.

"So now we've had it," Yancy said. "We have made our glorious football contribution to dear old Midwestern. We're through, pal, swept out the back door like a pile of trash."

"It sort of looks that way," admitted Clint, "except that. . . . Well, I've been thinking."

"Bully for you. You're lucky to have enough brains left to think with. Mine feel like scrambled eggs. So what have you been thinking?"

"That I'd like to play more football. If I didn't get

the urge knocked out of me today, it must be there for keeps."

"Your brains," said Yancy bluntly, "must be in worse shape than mine. Hasn't it sunk in yet, son? We're through."

"I won't admit it," Clint said stubbornly. "There's got to be a way—some way."

"How?" demanded Yancy.

Clint made an impatient gesture with his hand. "I don't know," he confessed. "I've got to think about it."

"You do that," Yancy said indulgently. "And let me know when you've got it licked."

Clint, despite his weariness, slept poorly when he got to bed that night. His mind kept racing, attacking an idea which, on the face of it, seemed hopeless, but which began to take the gradual form of an obsession. When he finally managed to bring some order to his thoughts he decided they were being motivated by three things: anger, stubbornness, and his unquenchable urge to play football.

His anger was directed at Midwestern's football policy. Understanding this, he tried to reason with himself, knowing that anger would only tend to cloud his thoughts when he forced them to the more important issues. The football policy was an established thing; he must accept it and recognize its logic.

The student squad, for instance, might possibly provide an occasional varsity prospect, but the cost of developing the potential of these men was more than the Athletic Department felt it could afford—too big a gamble. The money had already been spent in finding and recruiting players who had now proved themselves. They represented an investment which must be protected. The student squad was merely a gesture by which the university hoped to prove that all undergraduates would be given the chance to play football. Clint, knowing that he must accept this unpleasant fact, finally brought his anger under some control.

Logic also dictated the approach to his next step. He knew that men like himself, who wanted to play football, men who loved the game, should not be denied the privilege. He was not the only one. Those men of the student squad who had stuck it out to the hopeless bitter end were good examples. Clint knew they would feel just the same as he did about football.

The thought excited him until he ran into a dead end. Where could they play football? In a field outside of town or on a vacant lot? These were possibilities, of course, but hardly adequate for the magnitude of the idea which was growing in Clint's mind. Suddenly he had an inspiration. Jerking to a sitting position in his bed, he said aloud, "We just might pull it off!"

He aroused Yancy early in the morning, waiting

until Yancy had complained and groaned himself awake before giving him both barrels of the inspiration.

Yancy, still annoyed, let the idea sink in slowly. It grabbed hold suddenly, shaking him wide awake. "The old stadium?" he asked uncertainly. Then, with more conviction, he said, "Hey! I think you've got your teeth in something, boy!"

The old stadium was a relic of Midwestern's past, constructed in the days before football was a ruling force. It had been built in a depression at the edge of town, a spot selected for the contour, which provided a natural amphitheater, thereby holding building costs to a minimum. It had long since been abandoned in favor of the multimillion-dollar stadium, which was more accessible and had better parking facilities and a seating capacity five times as great.

"It still belongs to the University," Clint pointed out. "We'd have to get permission from the Athletic Department to use it."

Some of Yancy's enthusiasm drained away. "Yeah," he reflected soberly. "That's the gimmick, and a big one. It won't be easy. You're aiming pretty high."

"It's worth the chance. Let's go out and look it over."

"O.K.—that is, if I can walk. I feel awful."

"So do I. The exercise will do us good."

They ate a hasty breakfast and then started for the old stadium. When they arrived, their optimism suffered a setback. The field, unused for many years, was lumpy and overgrown with weeds. The single tier of concrete seats was crumbling in many places, returning to its original dust.

"What a mess!" said Clint. "Without big equipment it would take an awful lot of manpower to get that field in shape to play on."

"I get blisters just looking at it," Yancy said. "Let's look around for a nice vacant lot."

Clint shook his head. "This is the place for us if we can get it—a stadium of our own."

"O.K.," agreed Yancy, with a resigned shrug. "What next?"

"We've got to line up enough guys who want to play football as much as we do. Let's start with that. We won't hold out any hopes to them about getting this place. We'll just find out if they want to play—even on a vacant lot."

They set about the job of recruiting in the time they could spare from their classwork and homework. The effort was rewarding. Each man who had weathered the short, frustrating career of the student squad seemed eager to play more football—eager, at least, to prove to Midwestern's football officialdom that the game could not be limited to a chosen few. They were angry at the way they had been treated. Clint wondered just how long this anger would sustain them.

Clint's next job was one he would gladly have turned over to someone else—the job of asking the Athletic Director, Herbert Crawford, for permission to use the abandoned stadium. Clint knew Crawford only by reputation; he was said to be a hardheaded, aggressive businessman who did not want to be bothered with trifles.

Clint started for the Athletic Administration Building before he lost his nerve entirely, trying not to dwell on what he was about to try to do. It was not hard to imagine that Herbert Crawford would consider the request less than trifling, particularly when presented by a freshman still wet behind the ears. Clint had played with the notion of delaying his visit until after the football season, when things would be less hectic in the Athletic Department, but this bit of common sense had lost the battle to his impatience. He wanted to get the matter settled once and for all.

The palms of his hands were moist with nervousness as he entered the building and made his way toward Crawford's office. The door was open. He glanced gingerly inside and saw that the big man was protected by an outer office in which sat Crawford's private secretary, an angular and very efficient-looking woman. Clint was relieved to note that she was alone.

Gathering the last of his courage, he went in and stood uncomfortably while she ignored him to complete a few more lines of typing. The name plate on her desk told him she was Ms. Parnell.

She banged out the last period before looking up to study him with shrewd, appraising eyes. "Well, sonny," she demanded. "What's on your mind?"

This greeting robbed Clint of what little dignity he had mustered.

"I—I'd like to see Mr. Crawford," he blurted.

"You and ten thousand others," said Ms. Parnell, with more amiability than the words suggested. "He's a busy man, sonny. Maybe you'd better tell me what it's all about. That's what I'm here for—to give the bounce to anyone who might waste his time."

The last thing Clint wanted in the world was to discuss his new project with a secretary, yet he knew full well that Ms. Parnell would not give any ground. He made a vague movement toward the door.

"Let's have it, boy," she said, checking his indecision. "I'm not a dragon, no matter what they say about me."

He caught the amused glint in her eyes and felt a little more at ease. Before jumping in with both feet he drew a steadying breath. "I was a member of the student squad," he said. "We all want to play more football. I'd like to get permission to put the old field in shape. We'd do all the work, then use it to play football on."

He watched closely for Ms. Parnell's reaction. There was none visible to the naked eye. She swallowed the big dose without a flicker. "What's your name?" she asked.

"Clint Martin."

The poker look deserted her and the corners of her lips twitched. "Are you the lad who clobbered Bronco Slade?"

"Why . . . why, yes, I guess I am," Clint stammered. "How . . . how did . . ."

"Word gets around," she cut him short. "And now about this other business. Have you thought it all the way through?"

"No," Clint confessed. "I haven't."

"There's a lot to think about—proper uniform equipment to prevent accidents, proper coaching to prevent more accidents. Footballs, tackling dummies, other things—they all cost money, Clint. Where'll it come from?"

"I don't know. It's a new idea. I just figured that if we could get the field we could go on from there. Do you think we can get it?"

"Hard to tell. I'll talk it over with the boss."

Clint's face fell. "You mean that—"

"I mean *I'll* do the talking. He's a busy man. Now shoo! I'm also a busy woman."

Clint started for the door, dejection in his shoulders.

"Clint."

He turned around.

"The next man for you to see," said Ms. Parnell, "is Roger Grant, Director of Intramural Athletics. If anything comes of your idea, it will be under his jurisdiction. You'll find his office down the hall on the right."

Clint's optimism was running low as he started for Grant's office. He was reasonably sure, at this stage, that he was wasting time in the Athletic Administration building. He appeared to be getting the old runaround. Ms. Parnell had kept him from seeing the Athletic Director. She had passed the buck to Roger Grant, who would undoubtedly give Clint the final brush-off.

Clint shrugged. So what? he told himself. I've come this far. I might as well let them give me the works.

The door to Grant's office was also open. Clint went in, saw a man at a desk, and assumed that this person was merely another roadblock guarding the inner sanctum occupied by Grant. Midwestern took good care of its important people.

"May I see Mr. Grant?" Clint asked.

The man looked up from a letter he was reading. "Sure," he said. "You're looking at him."

Clint saw a blocky man with a broad good-natured face and close-cropped hair. Clint judged him to be in his middle thirties. There was something about Grant's relaxed air which seemed out of place in the hurly-burly atmosphere of early football season.

"I'd like to talk to you," Clint said. "That is," he added, "if you're not too busy."

"Ha," said Grant, grinning. "Let's not make jokes. I'm the baseball coach and director of intramural athletics. It's my duty to stay out from under foot while the football boys are scampering around. What's on your mind?"

"I'm Clint Martin, a freshman. I've got an idea I'd like—"

"Clint Martin?" interrupted Grant. "You're the kid that hung that nifty punch on Bronco Slade."

"Well, yes," Clint admitted, flustered. "I guess I am."

"Then you must be in the wrong office. You must be looking for the boxing coach."

"No, thanks." Clint grinned. "I like football better. That's what I'm here to talk about."

"Sit down and take your time," Grant invited him.

Clint eased himself into a chair and told his story,

as briefly as he could, encouraged by Grant's obvious interest. "And it seems to me," he concluded, "we ought to have a chance to play football if we want to."

"And I agree," said Grant, with strong conviction. "I asked for this intramural sports job because I firmly believe in it and am willing to work hard at it. I think that every one in school should be encouraged toward the kind of sport he likes and that the school should make every effort possible to make the facilities available. I guess I'm sort of a nut on the subject."

Clint, trying to subdue a mounting excitement, was now certain he had found the right man to help him with his project. "Then—then you think," he asked, a trifle breathlessly, "we might put this thing across?"

His hopes received a sudden chill when Grant, making an angry gesture with his hand, said, "I don't know. The cards are stacked against us. Enthusiasm is one thing; cold facts are another."

Clint waited, trying not to show his disappointment.

Grant shrugged. "Look, Clint," he said. "I like your idea; I like it fine. And for what it's worth, I'm going to do everything I can to help you put it across."

"Well, good!" said Clint, relieved. "That's fine."

"Don't get your hopes up. My guess is that Crawford will consider it a conflict of football interest, and his job is to see that all interest is focused on the Vulcans. I'll talk to Maggie. She's our best bet in this deal."

"Maggie?"

"Maggie Parnell, Crawford's secretary. She's been secretary to four athletic directors. She swings a lot of weight."

"I've talked to her," said Clint. "She sent me to you."

"So-o-o," mused Grant. "Was she interested?"

"She didn't say she wasn't."

"Good sign. We may have a chance, but don't get impatient. It may take time. She sometimes works that way. She probably invented the technique of brainwashing."

CHAPTER
5

It did take time, enough to build discouragement in Clint. Three weeks passed. The football season opened, with its customary hoopla, convincing Clint that his own pet project had been swamped in the excitement.

A few days later he was still nursing his disappointment, trying to accept the fact that his optimistic plans had turned into a pipe dream. He was crossing the campus on his way from class when he saw Maggie Parnell coming toward him. She was wearing a tweed suit and flat-soled shoes, striding in the manner of a person with a destination.

She stopped and said, without a build-up, "You can start work on the old field any time you want to." Then she waited patiently, while Clint absorbed the news.

"Well . . . well, thanks," he finally stammered. "He—he agreed to let us have it?"

Maggie nodded grimly. "I would have had a much easier job taking out his appendix with a nail file and a pair of pliers. He's still not sure what happened to him, so tread softly, Clint."

"I'll do my best." Then he added anxiously, "Have I put you on some sort of spot?"

"I've been on spots before. You're the one who's on one now. You'll work with Roger Grant. Good luck."

Clint walked several hundred feet on clouds before gradually coming back to earth. The first part of his dream—obtaining the old field—had become reality, but common sense told him that the remainder of the dream could easily contain a lot of nightmares. He took Yancy with him that afternoon on another visit to Roger Grant.

The problems seemed to multiply as they discussed them. Clint felt a hollowness grow inside him as he tried to face the cold facts Grant presented. He began to learn that playing football just for the fun of it was not as simple as it seemed.

Proper equipment for the safety of the men was essential. Such equipment, however, would cost money—lots of money, more than the players themselves could possibly afford, and Grant assured them that the Athletic Department would not contribute so much as a used shoelace. There was also the matter of tools to clear the field, even though Clint was assured that the players themselves would furnish the manpower.

It was suggested that the business community of Greenville might supply the needed funds, a suggestion which Grant brushed aside, pointing out that every fly-by-night organization on the campus always thought of that source first and that the merchants, who had been nicked hard and often, were gun-shy.

"No," agreed Clint gloomily, "you can't expect them to shell out forever without getting anything out of it for themselves, no credit, recognition, or—" his voice broke off with a grunt. He stared into space for a moment before announcing carefully, "Maybe I've got something. It may sound screwy, but it's worth considering."

The others waited curiously while Clint arranged his thoughts. "All businesses," he finally said, "pay for advertising and figure the money well spent. So why not appeal to them that way? Why not tell the owners that if they will outfit a single player the man will wear the name of their store or business on his jersey?"

Grant let out an appreciative whistle as Clint eased back in his chair, proud of himself. Reaching into his desk for some athletic equipment catalogs, Grant explained, "We might as well find out how much we'll have to ask for." He went through the pages from helmets to shoes, jotting down the prices as he went.

"A complete good outfit, though not the best," he announced, "will run close to eighty dollars. Footballs, the best—and I think it's economy to buy the best—will cost twenty dollars apiece. We'll plan to start with four."

"Whew," breathed Clint. "Sounds steep."

"It's not a poor man's game. However, I quoted retail prices and I'm sure I can get the university's usual discount on athletic equipment."

"That'll help," said Clint. "So now we put the bite on the businesses. Any suggestions as to where to start?"

An apologetic, almost guilty look came over Grant's face. "Yes," he confessed. "I'm afraid I have."

Clint hesitated cautiously before asking where.

"With Shoo-fly Finnigan."

"Who's he?"

Grant looked surprised. "I'd forgotten you haven't been here long," he said. "Maybe you've seen the man who rides a motor scooter in a derby hat with his coat tails flapping out behind him in the wind?"

"Yes, I've seen him. I thought he was some sort of nut. He's a traffic hazard, the way he drives that thing wide open. They ought to toss him in the slammer."

Grant cleared his throat before explaining pa-

tiently, "Shoo-fly Finnigan isn't quite the person anyone would care to toss into the slammer—not in this
town. He virtually owns it."

"*That* guy?"

Grant nodded. "He was born here. His first job, at
the age of six, so the story goes, was in a blacksmith
shop. He shooed the flies off horses while the blacksmith shoed 'em—no pun intended. That's how he got
his name."

"And then?"

"He grew up with the town and became a money-
making genius. He's the big wheel here in Greenville.
If he decides to play ball with us, the rest of the campaign should be a pushover."

"Does he like football?" Clint demanded.

Grant winced. "He hates it. Nobody knows quite
why, but it's the accepted belief that it's because Midwestern football represents a bigger business than he
runs himself. He has his pride, you know."

"Why don't *you* go to see him?" Clint asked hopefully.

"He associates me with the Athletic Department,
hence with football. Besides, I have a wife and fam-
ily."

Clint got up with a resigned sigh. "O.K.," he said,
"here goes. Yancy can sweep me off the pavement
when I get tossed out."

"A pleasure," Yancy said. "I want to be of *some* help in this business."

Clint consulted the telephone directory for the address of Shoo-fly Finnigan's office. His confidence was in poor shape when he and Yancy started out. Roger Grant's description of the local tycoon had not been reassuring.

They were both surprised at the location of Shoo-fly Finnigan's business headquarters. Instead of an impressive suite of offices in one of the modern buildings, the old man had been content to remain in a dilapidated building in a run-down section of the town.

"It's easy to see why the guy is rich," said Yancy. "He never spent any of his dough."

Shoo-fly's bright red scooter was parked along the curb. Clint was almost sorry to see this evidence that Shoo-fly was in residence. A small, weathered sign near the doorway of the building announced, *Finnigan Enterprises—Second Floor.* Clint solemnly shook hands with Yancy before starting up the stairs, which creaked beneath his weight.

Clint soon found the office he was seeking. The opaque glass on the upper half of the doorway was lettered *Shoo-fly Finnigan,* leaving no further doubt. Clint knocked gently on the glass.

After a brief silence a voice from inside called, "Come in!" It sounded as if someone had shaken loose gravel in a tin can. Clint turned the doorknob with a moist hand, opened the door, and entered cautiously.

The office was cluttered and dusty. Its occupant sat behind a desk, his back to the bright light from the window. Clint, squinting against the glare, could not see too distinctly. He got the impression of huge shoulders and an egg-shaped head, the latter illusion being caused by the round top of a derby hat. Beneath the hat he gradually made out a pair of formidable bushy eyebrows above two bright peering eyes.

"You didn't have to break the door down," Shoo-fly growled.

Clint swallowed. Before he could answer, Shoo-fly shot out, "Who are you and what do you want?"

Clint also took a little too much time to answer that one. Shoo-fly jumped in again. "No, don't tell me. I'll tell you. You're another student after money. I can spot 'em. Maybe you want to put up a monument to the first space monkey. Yeah, that's probably it. You want money, money, money. They always come to old Shoo-fly first."

Clint, sold as he was on his football project, was quickly getting fed up with this cantankerous old man. His eyes, becoming accustomed to the glare, informed him that Shoo-fly was enjoying the moment hugely, and Clint did not fancy himself, whatever the cause, as a target for Shoo-fly Finnigan's amusement.

Clint felt his face growing warm. "Do you want to hear what I've got to say, or don't you?" he demanded.

Shoo-fly's head came forward a trifle as if he was not entirely sure that he had heard correctly. "Well, now," he jeered, after a moment's thought. "Maybe I do and maybe I don't."

Clint's effort to keep his temper was, at best, half-hearted, so the effort failed. If Shoo-fly had intended to shake Clint's self-control, he was getting what he wanted.

Clint snapped, "Make up your mind! I haven't got all day!"

Shoo-fly's jaw sagged briefly. The force of his ensuing bellow almost blew Clint against the wall. "Who are you talking to, you young whelp?" he roared.

"I'm talking to *you!*" Clint yelled.

Clint was prepared for almost anything except the thing that happened. Shoo-fly leaned back in his chair. The corners of his mouth began an upward twist.

"Well," he said plaintively, "I just wanted to know. Nobody talks to old Shoo-fly like that any more. I guess they don't want me to have any fun. What's your name, boy?"

"C—Clint Martin," Clint managed to get out, trying to adjust himself to this new situation. The adjustment came hard. He subdued his anger cautiously, fearing a trap of some sort.

"Sit down, boy," Shoo-fly said. "Let's hear what's on your mind."

Clint eased himself gingerly into a straight-backed chair. He was still confused by Shoo-fly's sudden change of tactics, but he was reasonably assured of one thing, that beating about the bush would get nowhere with this tough old guy. "You were partly right about the handout," Clint said frankly. "And you'll like the second part of my proposition even less. It has to do with football."

Shoo-fly's head was thrust forward again and his eyes were fiery. Clint waited for an explosion, but it did not come. Shoo-fly was waiting with the alert caution of a man who recognized a capable opponent.

"Football," Clint repeated, letting the ominous word hang in the air. When nothing happened, Clint asked, "Shall I pack up and leave?"

Shoo-fly considered this a minute. Then he made a confession. "You've got a way with you, young man, of creating curiosity, and I happen to be the curious type. Keep talking, boy, but sit loose in your chair for a quick getaway."

Clint's next words were more or less inspired. He said. "There's an octopus at Midwestern—the Athletic Department. It's got a strangle hold on sport, on football in particular. A man can't play the game unless they say he can."

Shoo-fly made a sound beneath his breath. It sounded like an epithet. Whatever it was, it obviously gave approval to Clint's observations.

Encouraged, Clint bore down upon the theme, choosing his words carefully. "I'm probably a stupid, bull-headed guy," he said, "but I'm trying to buck the athletic organization. I think that the men who want to play football badly enough should have a chance to play the game, and that's what I'm trying to pull off. I need help, because I can't do it alone."

"Go on," said Shoo-fly, unwilling to commit himself without more facts at his disposal.

Clint told about having received permission to use the old stadium, stated his assurance that a number of nonrecruited football men were behind him, and mentioned Roger Grant's cooperation. He also outlined the idea of outfitting the players with billboard jerseys.

When he had finished, Shoo-fly said, "I'll go for it. But don't get me wrong. I hate football. It's played by a bunch of half-wits with nothing better to do than to bash in each other's skulls. However, I can't pass up this chance to toss a harpoon at the Athletic Department. Just pass the word that I'm willing to help you get a start, and I don't think you'll have trouble getting enough subscribers."

Shoo-fly waved off Clint's attempt to thank him. "Just show me you mean business," Shoo-fly said. "I own a contracting firm with enough big equipment to put that field in shape in a few hours. But it won't be that way. You kids'll clean it off by hand. I'll loan you shovels, picks, and rakes. I want to see acres of blisters, and when I see 'em I'll be pretty sure you boys want to play football bad enough to work for it. If I like the way you do the job I'll give you grass seed for it. Does that suit you?"

"Yes, sir," Clint said with a grin. "It suits me fine."

CHAPTER 6

With something tangible to offer, Clint and Yancy began a recruiting campaign of their own. It was a two-day job, but the results were satisfactory. Most of the candidates were former students who still felt that they had a lot of football in their systems. There was some grumbling, but most of the men felt that the end results would justify some honest labor.

The next step was another conference with Roger Grant, who helped Clint and Yancy to compile a list of the most influential business owners, particularly those who might be interested in the project. It was decided to limit the number to twenty-five.

"We could mess things up by being greedy," Grant pointed out. "We can only show a limited number of billboard jerseys in a game or scrimmage session, and with too many patrons wanting to see their ad in action we could just foul things up."

"There may not be enough uniforms to go around," objected Yancy.

"We'll face that problem when we get to it," said Grant. "And I can promise you there'll be plenty of other problems to face, too. Meanwhile, it ought to be easy to line up the first twenty-five patrons."

It was, as Grant had prophesied, a relatively easy job to obtain the backing of twenty-five Greenville businesses, largely because of Shoo-fly Finnigan. The mention of his name worked magic. The majority of them also seemed to think they would get their money's worth in advertising.

Clint then called the first meeting of the candidates. Twenty-eight of them showed up, gathering at one end of the huge dormitory lounge. They approved of the arrangement with the businesses, and agreed, without too much dissension, to contribute all the needed work. A work schedule which satisfied the majority, at least, was drawn up.

Work started on the old stadium a few days later. Shoo-fly Finnigan, true to his promise, had plenty of small tools on hand for the men to use. The men applied themselves with grim enthusiasm. The enthusiasm wore off fast, leaving only grimness.

It was a colossal task, made harder by the clumsy

efforts of the inexperienced men, who battled the strange implements until they learned the knack of using them. Clint, with the others, learned the hard way how to wield a hoe and how to master the technique of digging with a shovel. Nursing his sore hands and aching back, he was honestly amazed that the others kept at it as they did. There was some gold-bricking, to be sure, but it vanished promptly under the glares of the other men.

Clint, slightly mystified by the men's tenacity, came up with a solution he considered logical. There was usually an audience of some sort on hand. When word got around the campus that strange things were going on at the old stadium, many students came out to see for themselves. Once there they found the entertainment—the sight of suffering fellow creatures—to their liking.

The advice was free and generous. "Hey there, Williams, put a little more beef on that shovel handle!" or "Hey, Johnny, rest a little, will ya? You're getting me all tired out!"

The kidding, good-natured as it was, quite often held an undertone suggesting that the laborers were slightly feeble-minded to go to such great effort merely to play football, an implication which was not lost on the laborers. It aroused their stubbornness, keeping them at a job which had long since lost its attraction.

There was also another factor which, Clint reasoned, must have acted as a stimulus. The men were
often distracted from their work by the stutter of a
motor scooter. It was Shoo-fly Finnigan, of course, arriving at high speed, derby hat jammed down to his
ears and coat tails flapping in the wind.

He would park on the side line, sitting silently
upon the scooter while joy at all the anguish he had
caused flowed through him. There was something aggravating in his presence, in the jaunty air of power he
managed to convey. His attitude said, "This is all my
doing." He kept his head cocked in a sinister sort of
way as if trying to hear blisters pop. The men always
worked a little harder when Shoo-fly was on hand,
trying to prove, probably, that he could not beat them
down.

The project stirred something beyond amused interest on the campus. Clint, to his surprise, had some
more applicants for the labor squad, sophomores and
upper classmen, whose desire to play football was
strong enough so that they were willing to work for the
privilege. Clint explained to these men the problems
still ahead, chiefly that there would not be enough
equipment for everyone who might want to play. A few
of the men were discouraged by this. Others were more
than willing to take a chance and still others were
ready to supply their own equipment.

When the job was finally finished, Shoo-fly Finnigan was notified of the big event. He made quite a production of his inspection tour, tramping about the smooth field and grunting with disapproval when he found a chunk of dirt a little larger than he thought it should be. Clint, walking with him, began to get worried, a state of mind which Shoo-fly was undoubtedly trying to create.

When he walked back to his scooter he let his decision hang in space for a while. "All right," he said at last. "I guess it'll have to do. I'll send out the seed and loan you a seeder. I'll also send a man to show you how to do it so you won't waste seed."

Clint let out a relieved breath. "Thanks, Mr. Finnigan. Thanks a lot."

"Ugh," said Shoo-fly, starting his noisy motor to drown out any further demonstration.

When the football season ended and interest in the game subsided, it was not too hard for Clint to put his mind on other things. He found it somewhat of a relief to turn away from his football project temporarily. He had not realized, until now, how it had dominated his thoughts.

It was good to have more time for study and to move into the ordinary routine of college life, which was still a novelty to him. He found, to his surprise, that he had become a figure of minor importance on the campus, that his recent activities had made him known to the public and that he was claiming a bit more recognition than the average freshman. This was rather pleasant.

CHAPTER
7

Clint's holiday from the stress and worry of his project was short-lived. He received a visitor, Grady Bell, sports columnist for the leading local paper, whose reputation as a sports analyst was formidable about the campus. He was an angular, loose-jointed man in his early thirties.

Clint was frankly impressed and made no attempt to hide this. "Why, I read your column, Mr. Bell," he said.

"Make it Grady. Everyone else does." Clint liked the man's grin. "Maybe you've wondered why I haven't been around to see you sooner."

"To see *me?*" Clint was honestly bewildered. "Why?"

Grady's eyes narrowed as he studied Clint intently, wondering if he was being kidded. When he saw that he was not, his grin returned. "About this football deal you've stirred up. What else?"

"Sit down," said Clint, stalling for time to adjust his thoughts.

"I waited awhile," said Grady, "because—well, I probably felt the same as a lot of other people—that the idea wouldn't work out."

"It hasn't worked out yet. A dozen things could happen that would make it fall flat on its face."

"Nevertheless, it's developed to the point where I can't ignore it any longer. I'm district representative for a press association, so I'm going to write the story up and send it out."

"Do you *have* to?" Clint demanded, wondering why the idea frightened him.

Grady nodded. "Yes. If I don't, somebody else will. Another reason why I should be the one to do it is that I think it's a great plan and I won't ham it up. If I'm lucky enough to get the story on the wires it might pass the idea along to men in other football colleges like yours, and there are plenty of them not too far from here."

Surrendering to Grady's logic, Clint said grudgingly, "It doesn't look as if I have much choice. What do you want to know?"

"Just a few things," Grady said, pulling some

paper and a pencil stub from the side pocket of his coat.

Grady wrote the story and it clicked. The editors of the press association liked it. They sent it out across the country, with results that set a lot of wheels in motion.

Grady reported a small flood of letters from students in other schools who asked for more details on the subject. Some of the students in colleges within reasonable traveling distance of Midwestern went so far as to suggest a playing schedule between their makeshift teams.

"It's a great idea. Don't you think so?" Grady asked.

"I don't know what to think," Clint admitted with a worried frown. "Let's talk it over with Roger Grant."

Grant liked the idea too. "There'll be some bugs in it," he pointed out, however. "To start with, you'll need a coach, and I don't know where you'll get one. Some of the faculty members may have had coaching experience, but knowing Herb Crawford's coolness toward the project, they wouldn't dare stick their necks out. Furthermore, if there were any qualified coaches among the townspeople either Grady or I would know about it."

Grady confirmed this with a nod. "And if the

word got around that we needed a coach, we'd hear from a lot of crackpots, guys who've always wanted to coach football. A poor coach could do more harm than no coach at all."

"No coach at all suits me fine," said Clint, with a show of stubbornness. "The thought behind the whole thing is to have some fun out of football and not to be bossed around by someone who wants to make a reputation for himself. We'll get along fine by ourselves."

"Maybe," said Grant doubtfully. "Maybe not. We'll see. Meanwhile we'll let Grady set up the schedule. O.K., Grady?"

"Sure. You've got me hooked. I started the fireworks, so I might as well be stuck with the paperwork."

Studying came hard to Clint that evening. His brain would not cooperate. It was a labyrinth of thoughts stirred up by the recent meeting in Grant's office.

He was apprehensive, without understanding clearly why he should be. He knew only that his football project threatened to get out of hand. He had not planned it this way. He had wanted nothing more than to play football, any kind of football, with a bunch of guys who felt the same as he did. He had not planned on the confusing complications which were building up. Thinking about the future made his stomach flutter.

In discussing it with Yancy the next day, he demanded, "Am I chicken?"

"Undoubtedly," said Yancy. "But who isn't?"

"This thing excites me and scares me at the same time. I'm pretty sure I'd like to see it pan out, yet I can't help being afraid I've started a bulldozer at the edge of a cliff—something too big for me to handle."

"I guess you'd have to feel that way about it," said Yancy thoughtfully, "because everything has happened so fast. I also think that once you get used to the idea you'll get over being scared about it, and shift over to the thought that there are exciting days ahead."

"I hope you're right."

Yancy, to a large extent, *was* right. Clint's excitement and anticipation gradually crowded out his apprehension, as reports came in from Grady Bell that the movement, gathering speed, had obviously been established on firm ground.

It captured the fancy of men in other schools, men who were denied the privilege of playing their own mediocre brand of football; and in each instance some individual like Clint stepped forward to assume responsibility and to buck the odds. Clint learned that his own plan of business sponsors had been adopted by the other squads. Grady Bell, in a surprisingly short time, was able to announce a schedule of games for the following season.

The appearance of the schedule in his column created fresh interest on the campus. It was, for the most part, a friendly enough interest, in recognition of a pioneering experiment. Speculation as to the experiment's success was varied. Some prophesied a failure; others were more optimistic.

There was another faction too—a small one which had to be accepted if for no other reason than its nuisance value. It was composed of a dedicated group of scoffers. Its members' theme, available to anyone who cared to listen, was that Clint had started something very humorous and entertaining—like a circus, a free show open to the public where folks could come and laugh their heads off. Bronco Slade was obviously involved in the campaign.

One day on campus, Clint became aware of this. He was returning from a class when he saw Bronco, with several of his friends, loafing on the steps of the chemistry building. Clint checked his stride, glancing about for a possible detour. Finding none, he was half-inclined to retrace his steps with the annoyed air of a man who had forgotten something.

He abandoned the idea for two good reasons. In the first place, Bronco had already spotted him, as indicated by a swift word to his friends, whose attention also became centered on Clint. The second reason was equally good—a reluctance to give Bronco the impression that he was scared to face him.

When Clint met the group, Bronco said. "Hi, Clint."

"Hi," said Clint, maintaining his pace.

"What's your hurry?"

"No hurry," said Clint, forced to stop.

Bronco let the silence hang until Clint asked, "Got something on your mind, Bronco?"

"Just this and that," said Bronco, with a careless wave of his hand. "Uh, how about the big show you're planning to put on next fall?"

"Well, how about it?"

"I hear it'll be terrific, with all the clowns you'll have performing for you."

Bronco glanced at his friends for their approval. They chuckled dutifully. Clint felt the hair on his neck begin to prickle, a warning of the anger Bronco could so easily arouse in him. He fought against it, knowing this was not the place for it. Bronco was giving him the needle, making a deliberate attempt to make Clint lose his temper for the entertainment of the audience.

Clint managed a convincing chuckle of his own. "It ought to be a circus," he admitted. "Of course, we're not doing it to amuse anybody but ourselves. Just the same it's bound to be real funny."

Clint's grin was frank and open, as if he were sharing Bronco's fun. Bronco, however, was no longer having fun. Clint had snatched the ball from him, and Bronco was not quite sure how it had happened. His friends were grinning, too, in tacit appreciation of Clint's strategy. Their inquiring eyes were asking Bronco when he intended to get back into the game.

While Bronco was pondering the problem, Clint beat him to the punch again, with first-rate timing. "Well," he said cheerfully, "it's been nice seeing you." Then he turned and walked unhurriedly away.

He heard an involuntary guffaw from one of Bronco's friends, an answering groan from Bronco, then silence. Clint found himself perspiring mildly from the tension. He waited, however, until he had walked some distance before permitting himself to mop his forehead with a handkerchief. He had won another round from Bronco.

Clint's brainchild continued to develop smoothly. Foreseeable kinks were ironed out as well as possible. The merchants made their contributions and chose the design and color of the jerseys. It was agreed, however, that helmets must all be the same color, to avoid confusion on the field. Each school, it had been agreed, would use a different-colored helmet. When details of the billboard jerseys had been settled, Roger Grant ordered the equipment. There was nothing now to do but wait.

The wait was not as bad as Clint had anticipated. He studied hard, determined to have his grades in healthy shape by the end of his freshman year. Yancy followed Clint's example, and the time passed with surprising speed for both of them.

Yancy looked at Clint one day and said with some amazement, "You're growing up. You're putting on some extra meat."

"Yeah," said Clint. "It feels good, and I've still got room for plenty more."

"You might even be a man some day."

"I'll work at it."

The two friends went their separate ways at the close of school. Clint looked for a job—a particular sort of job, a laborer's job. He did not have far to look.

"So you want to build your muscles up," said Shoo-fly Finnigan. "I've got just the spot for you on one of my construction gangs. If you stick it out you'll be either a brute or a corpse."

Clint stuck it out. It could not be said that he became a brute, but the change in him was startling. He put on pounds of flesh, which developed promptly into muscle distributed nicely on his ample frame. His motions became more precise and accurate as the muscles worked in unison, giving him a coordination he had never before known. He wondered, with mounting eagerness, how the change would affect his football.

CHAPTER
8

Eagerness and curiosity were still high in Clint when school opened in the fall, and blended with these were recurring jolts of apprehension at what might lie ahead of him. The football project could no longer be relegated to his secondary thoughts. He would now have to meet it head on. He tried not to dwell upon the many things that could go wrong.

Yancy was impressed with Clint's appearance. "I do declare!" he marveled. "Where's that skinny guy I used to know? You're not the same guy who came to school a year ago."

"Not on the outside, I'm not. I've added about twenty pounds since then, and now I think I've leveled off."

"How's our stadium?" asked Yancy.

"Terrific. Looks like a park lawn. Shoo-fly kept it mowed this summer. He borrowed some fairway mowers from the golf club."

"Let's go look at it."

Clint had not exaggerated. The field was in great shape. They went to the small building at the end of the field, which had formerly been used to provide dressing quarters. Made of concrete blocks, the exterior of the building was in reasonably good shape. The corrugated-metal roof still looked waterproof, though it was rusted thin in spots.

The interior was, as they remembered it, a mess. The cement walls were scabrous with peeling paint. The cement floor, after years of neglect, was crumbling in spots. There was nothing, however, that could not be easily repaired.

The plumbing, at first glance, appeared unusable. Clint eased Yancy's discouragement on this point with the welcome information that one of the team sponsors was a plumber, who had assured Clint its condition was not as bad as it looked. The plumber had also agreed to patch the place up with secondhand material and to do the job at cost. It would not be too expensive to put the plumbing back in working order. Clint, by checking with the water department, had learned that there was still an open line to the old stadium.

There was still plenty to be done before football

could be started. Clint found this out when details started piling up on him. He was relieved to learn that the uniforms, with the exception of shoes, were safely stored in the basement of Roger Grant's home.

It had been previously decided that shoes, because of the important variation in size, should not be ordered with the other equipment. The men would be asked to play in sneakers until the squad had been shaken down to the twenty-five most promising players. Shoes for these men could then be ordered in exactly the right sizes.

There was bound to be some discrepancy in the sizes of the uniforms, but this was much less important than the proper fit of shoes. Uniforms could be traded among the men more readily than footwear.

It was necessary, now, to get in touch with all the players who had signed up for the squad and call them together for another meeting. This, in itself, was quite a task, because many of them had new addresses. When the players finally gathered, as before, in the lobby of the dormitory, the first item of business brought before the meeting was one which Clint had only casually considered.

A former student player said, "Look, Clint, don't you think this deal is far enough along for us to give ourselves a name?"

Thinking fast, Clint decided the suggestion was of

more importance than it first appeared to be. A name for the squad could easily impart a sense of unity, permitting both players and outsiders to refer to the squad as an established group which had already achieved its own personality.

"Good idea," said Clint. "Any suggestions?"

The same man said, "What's wrong with calling ourselves the Rebels? We are, in a way, staging a sort of rebellion."

There were nods and mutters of approval from the men.

"Sounds good to me," said Clint. "Any more suggestions?" There were no more. "All in favor of the name put up your hands." All hands went up. "O.K., we're the Rebels."

Further details were discussed. Clint told them the uniforms were ready to be handed out, but that more work had to be done first. There was enough money left from the original donations to buy lumber for the goal posts, the tackling-dummy standard, and benches for the locker room, which first had to be cleaned and painted. Work squads were soon assigned to the various jobs.

The work was finished with a promptness suggesting that the men were eager to get on to more interesting things. When the big day arrived, the Rebels gathered in the locker room, avidly eying the pile of boxes containing uniforms. Clint had to forestall an undisciplined rush in their direction.

It was a problem he did not care to face. There were new uniforms for no more than half the men. Twelve of them, Clint noted with relief, had equipped themselves with well-worn outfits which, however, appeared to be adequate. The men left without uniforms might present a problem.

"Take it easy," Clint called out, as the pile began to attract the men like a magnet. "I told you at the meeting there wouldn't be enough uniforms to go around, and that the only thing I could figure out was to give first chance to the men who went out for freshman football. Some of you guys may rate an outfit more than they do. That's something we'll find out later."

The first show of dissension raised its head when one of the men said irritably, "How'll we ever find it out if we don't have clothes to play in?"

Clint felt a chill along his spine. Friction of one sort or another, he had known, was bound to come, and inevitably he would find himself in the middle of the resulting hassle. Well, here it was—the first one. He could not back away from it. He hauled in a deep breath, trying to think of a diplomatic answer.

Before he could form the words, another voice spoke up. "Aw stow it, Rex! We all knew what to expect before we came out here. We also knew what Clint was up against. He can't hand-feed all of us, and if that's what we expect we have no business being here. If we don't like the setup we can quit any time we want to."

There were mutterings of assent. Clint let out his breath, grateful for the reprieve. He had weathered his first encounter without loss of face, but he knew very well that he might not be as lucky next time. He read off the list of men for whom the uniforms were intended and the attack upon the pile began.

It developed swiftly into a happy sort of madhouse, with the jerseys supplying fuel for the hilarity. The businessmen had gone hog-wild, making the most of this big chance to advertise their product and themselves. Restricted only by the limits of their imagination they had trampled down artistic barriers in favor of the gaudiest eye-catchers they could think of. They thought up some dandies, and the Rebels loved them.

Their approval was so great, in fact, that several good-natured tussles started over some of the choicer items. The tussles were accompanied by loud demands.

"Aw, come on, Bert, give me that Gandy Fish Market job! That lobster on it goes with my complexion!"

"You oughta let *me* have Oglethorp's Auto Parts!

I'm a little nearsighted and those neon headlights on the front might help."

And so it went on, until all arguments were settled or, more accurately, until the proper sizes were traded around to fit the proper men. Clint ended up with a creation studded with gold stars against a purple background, leaving room, fore and aft, for the glittering replica of a diamond ring from Clifton Jewelers.

Yancy was happy with his lot, a Parker Bakery horror, tempting its viewers with a big doughnut front and rear. His only beef was that they had forgotten the cup of coffee.

The merriment in the dressing room, Clint noted critically, began to be a bit prolonged. The gags began to lose their spontaneity as if the men were trying to think up new wisecracks, in a deliberate effort to kill time. Clint sensed the reason. The jerseys, though entertaining enough in private, were nevertheless pretty wild affairs, which could easily make the Rebels feel uncomfortably self-conscious. The men were feeling extremely doubtful as to how the public would receive them. Clint made no attempt to hurry them along. He merely waited until the men themselves accumulated enough courage to face the outer world.

When they left for the field, a protective grimness settled over them. Clint had expected a few curious spectators, because word was bound to have leaked out that this was the day when the butterflies would emerge from their cocoons. He was not prepared, however, for the crowd that was on hand to greet the Rebels. It appeared, almost, to have been arranged, as if someone had assumed the self-appointed job of a Paul Revere to spread the news about the campus. Shoo-fly Finnigan, in his usual aloof manner, was sitting on his scooter, parked along the side line.

When the Rebels paraded on the field, the audience cut loose, raucously delighted with the fantastic display of billboard jerseys. Clint estimated the gathering roughly at some two hundred fans, if you could call them that.

The Rebels, having expected something of the sort, weathered the first barrage of comments rather well, even though symptoms of annoyance were beginning to appear. Clint, feeling that any organized form of practice would be hopeless under these conditions, handed out the footballs and let the men shift for themselves.

It appeared to be a sound idea. The Rebels divided into groups, some running signals in a disjointed sort of way, others merely passing or booting the ball around. They were controlling their embarrassment and aggravation well enough to keep out of trouble, until a curious change began to appear among the crowd.

The razzing at the start had been more or less good-natured, but some of the remarks were changing now, developing unnecessary sting and crudeness. It puzzled Clint until he gradually became aware of what was going on—a normal enough display of the diversity of human nature.

He understood that in a crowd of this size there were bound to be people unrestricted by moderation and good taste. One wisecrack led to another. When someone came out with a remark that drew a laugh, it served as an immediate challenge for someone else to top it with a smarter gag. It became a contest which grew louder, cruder, and more unrestrained.

A worried tension started to build up in Clint. He noted that the worst offenders were gradually forming their own group as if following the magnetic pull of common interest. They were aided in this by the majority of the fans, who, not wishing to be associated with the vulgarity of the few, began to edge away, leaving the more boisterous element to have its fun alone.

Clint's alarm began to mount as the hecklers stepped up the pressure. The unwarranted, vicious needling was reaching him. It was also rasping dangerously on the raw nerves of the other Rebels. Clint could see the anger building in them, rapidly approaching the hair-trigger stage. It began to look as if the hecklers had stretched their luck too far.

The danger of the moment sent Clint into action. The Rebels were his responsibility. He stifled a quick surge of panic at the thought of what could happen if the Rebels lost their heads. He worked fast, pleading with them not to blow their tops.

He might have pulled it off. He was making progress, when a diversion from an unexpected source blew his good intentions to smithereens. A loud bellow, easy to locate, drew his attention to the side line. Shoo-fly Finnigan had had enough. He cut loose with a roar that rose above the racket of the hecklers. Then, determined to make his point more forcibly, he abandoned his scooter and headed for the field, making good speed on his short legs.

He planted himself before the nearest man and expressed himself until his derby joggled. His terms were picturesque and pointed, probably learned while shooing flies from horses. An impulsive cheer came from the fans who had decided to behave themselves, and the cheer quite possibly forced the man in front of Shoo-fly into a careless demonstration. He put a hand against the old man's chest and shoved. Shoo-fly's heels caught in the turf and he sat down hard.

Shoo-fly's contact with the ground had the same effect as tossing a lighted match into a pool of gasoline. The Rebels needed an excuse, however small, to release their pent-up anger. They may have justified themselves in a vague way by feeling that they were going to the aid of a helpless old man. At any rate, whatever the stimulus, it was all they needed to release their rage.

Yancy, with a snort of fury, made the first break toward the hecklers, gaining a negligible head start as the rest of the Rebels closed in fast behind him like a colorful avalanche. Some of them ran grimly. Others went into battle with glad yells.

Clint knew a moment of quick horror, knowing full well how an outbreak of this sort could affect his plans. This, he thought, with a stab of anguish, could easily be the beginning and the end of the Rebel project.

Even as these thoughts rushed through his mind Clint found himself charging with the rest. There was no way to control the Rebels at this stage and Clint was guilty of a tingling gladness that he was helpless to control them. The barbs had penetrated Clint's hide, too, arousing a wrath that had to be released through action.

The attack was so spontaneous and swift that the hecklers had no chance to run—even had they wanted to. There were plenty of them who obviously had no intention of retreating. Encouraged by the fact that the

Rebels were outnumbered, the more hardy of the hecklers could not doubt the outcome of the fight. They held
their ground and started slugging. The uncertain ones,
afraid to run for fear of being tagged as chicken, stuck
around to prove their bravery.

Clint, squaring off with the first man to oppose
him, found that he was facing a man whose height and
weight were equal to his own. Moreover, judging by
his stance and his maneuvers, he had had previous
boxing experience. He lost no time in demonstrating
this. His left hand kept flicking out to jar against Clint's
nose. Clint grunted with the pain. He tasted blood, then
let his temper get away with him, uncorking a couple
of wild swings which whistled harmlessly through
space. Another roundhouse missed, leaving him wide
open for a sizzling left hook, which might easily have
put the lights out had it landed on the button. Luckily,
it landed high, carrying enough force, however, to send
Clint to the ground.

Clint came up fast, only slightly dazed. He shook
his fuzziness away and came in with more caution,
deciding belatedly to quit acting like a chump.

The other, with a mean grin, feigned surprise.
"Still looking for more, sucker?" he demanded.

Clint was in no mood for conversation. He had no
time for it, anyway. The big guy followed his words
with a swift rush and blasting right hook designed to

settle matters once for all while Clint was still hazy from the knockdown.

Clint, however, was not as groggy as he seemed. He ducked beneath the blow, with his legs well braced for a thundering wallop to his opponent's midsection. He slammed it in, and the heckler's breath came out with a loud *woosh.* His legs buckled as he sat down, looking stupid.

Clint repeated the man's question. "Still looking for more, sucker?"

The other merely glared, fighting for breath until he regained enough to get back on his feet. Clint, watching him, had sense enough to read the warning flicker in his eyes. When his foot lashed out in a savage kick Clint swerved in time to let the shoe glance off his thigh.

It was the heckler, this time, who should have read the warning. Clint moved back a stride or so, experiencing sharp pleasure that his opponent had set the terms of the encounter. The fellow was bringing his leg back for another kick when Clint nailed him with a savage tackle, crashing him to the ground with enough force to knock out his remaining wind. He lay there gasping, pale and twitching, with no more fight left in him.

Clint now turned his attention to other things. There was plenty to attend to. One of the most classic brawls in the history of Midwestern was at its height. Men battled, prone and upright. The hecklers were fighting like cornered rats, and the Rebels were hard pressed.

Clint turned his attention to a Rebel who was being attacked by two men. Clint peeled one of them off, spun him around, and cooled him with a solid right to the jaw. He found other work to do, accumulating bruises as the time passed pleasantly.

How long it lasted, he could only guess—probably for quite a while, because when the Rebels were gradually gaining the upper hand they were robbed of glorious victory by a rude and very wet interruption.

Someone, obviously, had had the common sense to put in a riot call from the nearest phone. The authorities, with some experience along these lines, wasted no time in taking action. The fire department played the biggest role. The fire fighters ran a pair of hoses from the nearest hydrant, aiming powerful streams on friend and foe alike.

The brawl did not last long after that. There is nothing like a violent jet of chilly water to cool tempers and reduce the truculence of fighters. When the combatants had been sloshed about the field by the force of the water and had skidded here and there, there was little fight left in them. The hecklers left in soggy shoes, while the battered Rebels made their dripping way back to their dressing room. Their first practice session was over for the day. It had been more spectacular than they had planned.

CHAPTER 9

Clint joined the Rebels in their soggy trek. The fire hose had subdued his lust for battle. The excitement of the moment drained away, to be replaced by something colder than the water from the hose—an understanding of the consequences which might possibly result. The facts stood out in all their stark reality.

Most of the Rebels appeared to be following the same line of thought. A few halfhearted wisecracks failed to bring response. The men, for the most part, were thoughtful and subdued, knowing they had put some formidable wheels in motion. One of them had the temerity to ask, "What happens now?" He was answered by vague, worried shrugs.

On the way back to the dormitory Yancy's customary optimism failed him. "I'm scared," he admitted honestly to Clint.

"So am I. We may have put the skids under ourselves before we had a chance to get started. We'll find out tomorrow, that's for sure."

Clint's prophecy was accurate. The bomb dropped when Clint attended his first morning class. The instructor, meeting him in the doorway, delivered the message. Clint was to report immediately to the office of the dean, Dr. Prescott.

Clint nodded, trying to control the bleakness of his thoughts. His knees felt like jelly as he approached the office. He pulled himself together to the best of his ability before entering. In the outer office was a young, efficient-looking woman, the Dean's secretary. Clint gave his name.

The secretary said, "Doctor Prescott is expecting you." She touched the lever of the intercom and announced, "Mr. Martin is here to see you, sir."

The responding words sounded ominous to Clint. "Send Mr. Martin in."

Clint stiffened his back as he entered the large corner room. He experienced a brief impression of luxury, restful colors, a deep soft rug, fine paintings on the walls, and expensive leather-covered furniture.

His interest, however, was chiefly centered on the

occupant of the chair behind the huge mahogany desk, an angular man with sparse hair, a high forehead, and dark, thoughtful eyes. There was a quiet air of self-control about the Dean, the air of a man who expected almost anything, and usually found it, in his daily problems.

"Sit down, please, Mr. Martin," he said.

Clint eased himself into a leather chair beside the desk.

The Dean came promptly to the point. "Let's hear your version of what happened yesterday," he said.

Clint hauled in a deep breath, hoping to control a voice he feared might be a trifle shaky. "A crowd razzed us from the side line," he said. "We lost our heads. I guess you know the rest."

Dr. Prescott nodded slowly. Clint hoped he read approval in the nod—approval of Clint's frankness. The Dean shot a swift glance at Clint's mouse-colored eye, saying dryly, "Yes, I know the rest." He remained thoughtful for a moment, staring at the wall.

Clint furtively wiped the moisture from his forehead.

The Dean suddenly turned dark, serious eyes on Clint. "I cannot risk the recurrence of such a disgraceful performance. You understand that, don't you, Mr. Martin?"

"Yes, sir," said Clint dully.

"You may find this a close distinction," the Dean went on, "but your football squad, the Rebels, must be accepted by the university as an organization which has assumed the proper responsibility for such a group. The men who razzed you have not declared themselves as an organization, which means that they, if they overstep the bounds, must be punished individually. On the other hand, I have the authority to disband or outlaw any organization which I may consider to be an irritating factor likely to cause trouble. Do you follow me?"

"I think so, sir. You mean that the Rebels, even if we don't cause any trouble ourselves, may stir up enough resentment among other people to make you feel we're a bad influence, and that we ought to be eliminated."

"Exactly. I am the one who has to make the decision."

"Yes, sir."

"You failed to give me a true picture of what happened yesterday."

Ignoring Clint's look of protest, the Dean continued. "You have a powerful ally, Shoo-fly Finnigan, who has already been in touch with me and who has accepted the responsibility for touching off the fireworks. He has also pointed out to me," the Dean added, with a rueful smile, "that many of the most influential sponsors are actively concerned with your project, and it is our own strong policy to maintain the best possible public relations with everyone in Greenville."

The muscles in Clint's throat relaxed a bit. His expression of hope, though cautious, was not lost on Dr. Prescott.

"There are strings attached," he told Clint promptly. "I must make certain stipulations for the good of the school. Specifically, if the Rebels are directly responsible for more trouble of a violent nature, such as yesterday, they will be disbanded. Is that clear?"

"Yes, sir. But—but what if we are not the ones who start it?"

"I will make this concession. You are always privileged to protect yourselves, and the men who start the trouble will definitely be dealt with through this office."

"Thank you, sir."

"I don't think you'll find it easy. If I know my undergraduates, you will be subjected to more razzing, but that is something we cannot attempt to control unless it becomes offensive to the public. In that event we'll take prompt action. However, if the Rebels permit themselves to be razzed into another brawl, there will be no more Rebels."

"That's more than fair, sir," Clint said, rising. "I think I can promise you that we'll behave ourselves."

"I hope so," said the Dean, offering his hand. "Your project is unique, and I believe it would be helpful to the university. It deserves success. Good luck."

Clint left the office with the buoyant feeling of a man who has escaped an ugly fate. The feeling lasted until certain aspects of the situation took form in his thoughts, at which point his buoyancy began to be replaced by worry.

He was still willing to admit that the Dean's concession, considering the circumstances, had been generous, but it gradually became obvious to him that the Dean had placed the Rebels on a dangerous spot, like that of a man with a sword hanging by a single hair above his head.

It had been easy enough for Clint to make the impulsive statement that the Rebels would behave themselves. But what actual assurance did he have to back the statement? None at all. The men, he was convinced, would try to keep their tempers under wraps. They would be full of good intentions. But how long would good intentions last in a group of men with varied dispositions, different boiling points, and questionable resistance to the further needling that was bound to come? A single slip-up, just one unintentional loss of temper by any of the Rebels, could write an end to their existence as a football squad. Clint's palms grew clammy at the thought.

When Clint told Yancy about the interview with Dr. Prescott, Yancy's first reaction was the same as Clint's had been. "Yea, boy! That's great!"

"Think it over," Clint suggested.

Yancy thought it over, grew sober, and said, "Ouch!"

"We haven't even started," Clint said bitterly. "Before we've had a chance to hold a single workout we've got a shotgun pointed at our heads."

Clint explained the situation carefully to the Rebels when they gathered in the dressing room that afternoon. He was relieved to find that they accepted their new and precarious position seriously, grateful that the Dean had given them another chance. They were subdued and watchful as they headed for the field.

Clint experienced an uneasy moment upon seeing the number of fans gathered for the occasion. There were more than on the previous day, a natural enough result of the entertaining show which had been staged the day before. The fans were hoping for a repeat performance.

Clint soon learned, however, that there was no cause for undue alarm—not yet, at any rate. The hecklers were not in evidence. Clint hoped, uncharitably, that most of them were still in dry dock for repairs. It appeared, however, that the Rebels could enjoy a short reprieve from their enemies, not that Clint expected the reprieve to last.

There was kidding, of course, quite a lot of it, good-natured for the most part. The Rebels, though selfconscious, managed to absorb it without any dangerous show of anger. They divided into groups, as on the previous day, and started to enjoy themselves. Clint had had no chance the day before to start his own workout. He found a spare ball now, and Yancy, sensing his intention, broke downfield. Clint heaved the ball to him.

It was the first pass Clint had thrown this year and its effect on him was rather startling, in a way that puzzled him at first. There was nothing spectacular about the pass, yet it created a weird tingling which was slow in leaving him.

The tingling had started with the first feel of the ball, almost as if he had never felt a ball before. It fitted his hand with a perfection he had not known in the past, and the ball had left his hand with a smooth precision he could not explain.

"Let's try a few more," he told Yancy, trying to subdue his eagerness.

Yancy nodded. "I think I know what you mean."

They tried some more, Clint to Yancy, at varying speeds and distances.

Yancy finally came back grinning. "Now I'm sure I know what you mean," he said.

"What happened?" Clint demanded, filled with excitement.

Yancy shrugged. "What's so mysterious about it? A year ago you weren't more than a gangling kid, and you coordinated like a kid. You've put on almost twenty pounds, in the right places. Now your brain can tell your muscles what to do and they'll go ahead and do it."

The two discussed the workout in Clint's room.

"Well," said Yancy drily, "the boys had fun, at any rate."

Clint caught the meaning behind Yancy's tone. "A little too much fun," he agreed.

"Isn't that the idea behind it all?"

"You don't have to spell it out for me," Clint answered gruffly. "If we let them use that place for a playground we're setting them up for slaughter when we get around to scrimmage. Most of them are soft as mush. They've got to be hardened up."

"And so?"

Clint sighed. "Yeah, I know. It's up to me. I wonder how they'll take it."

He laid it on the line the following afternoon, before the Rebels left the dressing room. "This thing has developed farther than I expected when I first came up with the idea. At that time I figured we could just fool around and do more or less what we wanted to. That's all been changed by the games we've scheduled. We've got to get in shape, not necessarily to win the games but to keep ourselves from getting hurt. Does that make sense?"

There were nods of agreement.

"O.K., then. We can't treat our workouts like picnics. We've got to do calisthenics. It'll be work, not fun. I can't make any of you go through with it if you don't want to. You can take as much as you want to or lay off when you want to. It's up to you."

There were no objections. Clint breathed a little easier, but only till the Rebels started for the field. The hecklers were on hand, looking somewhat the worse for wear but clearly determined to take up where they had left off a couple of days before. As soon as the Rebels appeared, their enemies cut loose with loud assorted gibes. Clint saw the expressions of anger that appeared on the faces of his men.

He sensed the hecklers' purpose. Word of Dr. Prescott's ultimatum had undoubtedly leaked out, providing an excellent incentive for them, a made-to-order chance to collect full payment for the beatings they had taken. They hoped that they could wreck the Rebels permanently, merely by the use of patience and a lot of lung power. If a single Rebel could be pushed beyond his limit, needled to the point of starting trouble, the hecklers' mission would have been accomplished.

Clint swallowed a scared lump in his throat. "They're trying to make us start another brawl," he warned the men. "If we do we're through." There was nothing more to say.

He started his men on their calisthenics. It was a precarious situation, balanced on a needle. Clint's stomach almost turned over as he saw Rebel after Rebel reach the snapping point, then pull himself to safety with a mighty effort.

Shoo-fly Finnigan was once more on the side line sitting stone-faced on his scooter. He posed another threat. Would the hot-tempered old guy blow his top again? It was a needless worry. Shoo-fly had learned his lesson. He behaved himself.

The calisthenics proved a big help to the Rebels, giving them a chance to work off the violence they might otherwise have directed toward the hecklers. They sweated, strained, and grunted, using their energy in the safest way they knew.

The workout ended without disaster. It was touch and go at times, but the Rebels weathered the ordeal nobly. When they left the field, it was with a touch of swagger. They knew they had won another fight the hard way. Clint was exhausted, more from tension than from exercise.

CHAPTER 10

The hecklers were not easily discouraged. They continued their campaign, stepping up the tempo as they tried to crack the Rebels' self-control. They came within a hairsbreadth of succeeding several times, but the margin, though slim, remained in favor of the Rebels.

They managed, to their credit, to build a protective shell about themselves. The hecklers, in their efforts to break through the shell, flirted dangerously with public tolerance and had sense enough to pull their horns in when the other fans began to mutter angrily.

At the end of a comparatively peaceful day on the field, Yancy said hopefully, "Looks like we've got 'em licked."

"That was only the first skirmish," Clint said with conviction. "There'll be more."

"What makes you think so?"

"Because it figures. A bunch of guys who would sound off as they did in the first place must have one thing in common—a mean streak. It's the sort of thing that could pull them together in the beginning and hold them together after they get slapped around a bit. They won't quit. We knocked the daylights out of them in the brawl and we've made them look silly these last few days. The slobs have their pride, you know. Besides, the Rebels are now a challenge to them and they hate our guts more than they did before. We'll see more of them."

Clint did his best in the following days to weld the Rebels into a football unit. It was a big job, becoming bigger and more demanding as the days went on. The Rebels had a scant three weeks to prepare for their opening game, and their progress, by any standard, was disheartening.

Clint felt compelled to accept the blame for this. "I'm not a coach," he told Yancy in a moment of discouragement. "To start with, I don't know enough about football, and to make things worse I'm not a slave driver. I just don't seem to have what it takes to order men around when I have no authority over them, and particularly when they know very well that I don't know what I'm doing."

Clint kept trying with the help of Roger Grant and Grady Bell to find a coach, but it was a futile search. Faculty members who had had previous coaching experience were wary of offering their services, not wishing to antagonize the powerful Athletic Department. Grady Bell, although in close touch with the townspeople, was unable to find a suitable man to undertake the job. Clint even gave the Rebels themselves a chance to volunteer, but none of them was willing to accept the responsibility.

One of the few breaks to come the Rebels' way took place on an early day of practice. A volunteer appeared unexpectedly to solve one of Clint's major problems.

It was a student, who approached Clint on the field. He introduced himself. "My name's Clem Davis. I figured maybe you might need a trainer to do a little patchwork on the boys."

"You bet we do," said Clint.

"I'd like the job." Seeing Clint's quick expression of alarm, the newcomer explained, "I'll work for free. I'm strong for this thing you've started, and I'd like to help."

"Well, that's great," said Clint, with a touch of uncertainty which Clem promptly eliminated.

"I think I'm qualified," he said. "I'm a pre-med here at school, and I had first-aid training in the Navy."

"Man, you've got a job." Clint accepted his offer gratefully. "And I hope you don't run into anything but patchwork."

"I hope so too," said Clem.

In this respect the Rebels continued to be lucky. The usual minor injuries developed, but none presented a serious problem to Clem's deft fingers.

It was not Clem's fault that the squad gradually began to decrease in size. It was a situation Clint had sensibly anticipated, yet when it became evident he found it disappointing and hard to face, despite the fact that it formed a logical pattern. The men, even with their mere smattering of football, still knew enough about the game to realize that the Rebels, as a football team, would present no threat to the average high school squad, and that the success of the movement would probably be determined by the showing the Rebels made in their scheduled games.

Added to this was the daily grind of training, a disillusionment to those who had come out for a playful romp. Tactful as Clint tried to be, he had had to bear down at times, thereby learning that certain men disliked the pressure. These men lost their love of football and returned to easier pursuits. The lack of uniforms and equipment was another reason for the diminishing squad.

In this connection, Clint was faced with another

tough decision. It was inevitable that some of the men should begin to stand out above the others. Some of them possessed natural talent, which developed as the days went on. Others worked harder to make up for the ability they lacked. A few of the outstanding men were those who had furnished their own outfits. These men deserved the newer billboard uniforms more than some of the men who wore them. It was a delicate, touchy situation which kept Clint worrying before he worked out a solution. He laid it on the line again before the squad.

After explaining the problem, Clint said, "Maybe I'm chicken, fellows, but this is a decision I don't intend to make. This isn't *my* squad, it's yours. We went into it with that idea. We're going to vote on it—secret ballot. You guys know as much about it as I do, so I'm going to ask you to write down the names of the twenty-five men you think should wear the new uniforms. Make your lists and give them to me tomorrow in sealed envelopes. Appoint a committee of three men to go over the lists and compile the result. Does that sound fair?"

The men considered Clint's suggestion soberly and agreed that it was fair. One of the men brought up a pertinent point. "There could be a tie vote, Clint— maybe several of them. What happens then?"

"I thought of that. We'll toss a coin."

The Rebels agreed to this and went about the serious business of readjusting the squad by means of a secret ballot. The operation was successful, but the shock to the patient was considerable. A few of those eliminated from the first string couldn't take it. They quit the squad.

Then a man by the name of Max Hacker was another of Clint's problems. It was a minor problem, at the moment, but one that could conceivably cause trouble. Max Hacker was a sportswriter. Working for the other Greenville daily paper, he considered himself a rival of Grady Bell—probably because Grady was a better analyst and writer. Whatever the reason, Hacker kept himself in a constant lather in his effort to oppose Grady's opinions whenever he felt he had a leg to stand on. Grady was pulling for the Rebels. Hacker, as a matter of principle, pulled against them.

He harped on two main themes, both fairly logical. Why, he pondered in his column, should the university go along with the ambitious program of the Rebels? He tentatively conceded that the original idea might have merit so long as it remained intramural. Beyond that point, he expounded at some length, it would be a travesty on football, a mockery of a proud sport when the fans gathered for the sole purpose of laughing their heads off at the clumsy antics of two untrained teams.

Max Hacker's second theme, which was more realistic, was the one which made occasional cold shivers travel up Clint's spine. Hacker kept yapping on the subject of injuries. He called the attention of his public to the risks involved when inexperienced men, without proper supervision, were exposed to the dangers of modern football.

"The trouble is," Clint said anxiously to Yancy, "the guy's got a point."

"I guess he has," said Yancy. "Except that he doesn't bother to call attention to the injuries on the varsity and freshmen squads."

"Oh, that's different," Clint said dryly. "You're forgetting that those boys are getting hurt in the line of business. It's an occupational hazard. The Rebels, on the other hand, are merely supposed to be having fun."

"I stand corrected."

"We've been lucky, up to now—mighty lucky. This boy Hacker is acting like a shyster lawyer chasing an ambulance, hoping for a nice messy accident he can crow about in his column."

"Let's hope he doesn't get it."

The Rebels' games against outside schools were scheduled for Friday afternoons, and the opening game, against the Castoffs of Rutland Tech, came upon Clint much too soon. The Rebels, he was certain, were not ready for the test.

Clint had done his best, knowing all the time that his best was far from adequate. He lacked a sound foundation of football knowledge and experience. It was an undeniable fact, one which the Rebels understood without resentment. They, too, had done their best, and unlike Clint, many of them were optimistic, basing their optimism on the belief that the Castoffs, having been saddled with similar handicaps, would be no better than the Rebels.

The game drew a sizable crowd of fans, a development which did not take Clint by surprise. The novelty of the thing possessed considerable drawing power. The majority of the fans were there for kicks. They were in a circus mood, expecting to be entertained, not thrilled.

The Castoffs contributed their share of entertainment before the game got under way. Their jerseys were also wild and colorful. The fans enjoyed them. The men guffawed and the women shrieked with delight. Everyone was glad to have come.

The problem of officials for the game was solved with the grudging cooperation of the Athletic Department, which permitted Grant himself to act as referee and other qualified men to fill the posts of umpire, field judge, and linesman.

The Rebels tried to look impressive in their warm-up. Instead, they were nervous and butterfingered. The

Castoffs, in Clint's eyes, looked considerably better, and the reason for this was apparent. They had a coach, an older man who looked as if he knew his business.

Clint gathered brief consolation from the fact that the Rebels seemed to have a weight advantage. He told himself that the Rebels, obviously confident, might turn this confidence to their advantage. It was nothing but a flight of fancy, as Clint soon learned when the game got under way.

The Castoffs won the toss, electing to receive. It was a wise choice. They ran the kickoff back to their own forty-eight-yard line behind good blocking. The overeager Rebels grabbed at shadows and floundered in each other's way. Four running plays followed by a short pass into the end zone scored a touchdown. The Castoffs kicked the extra point to jump into the lead, 7-0.

The Rebels then had their chance to go on the offensive. They brought the kickoff back to the twenty-four-yard line, where Clint tried to fire up some sort of an attack. It was hardly recognizable as such. He sent the Rebels through their simple plays, which posed no great problem for the Castoffs. The Rebels struggled for four yards in three downs. They kicked on the fourth down. Clint booted a fine punt, which merely served to delay the Castoffs a little longer on their march to another touchdown.

There was no more false confidence in the Rebels. It was replaced, fortunately, by a shamed anger, which was somewhat more effective than their confidence. Taking advantage of the change, Clint was able to tighten the Rebels' defense a bit, and to grind out an occasional first down on the offense. By comparison, however, it was not much of a performance, and the matter of comparison was the aggravating, hopeless factor.

Little as Clint knew about football, he knew that, man for man, the Rebels were as good as or better than the Castoffs. They were bigger, just as fast and they had as much courage. They merely lacked experience, proper coaching, and the close-knit unity that comes from knowing what each teammate is supposed to do.

It was not that the other team was really good—far from it. The Castoffs committed many blunders and at times looked pretty silly. It was just that the Rebels committed more blunders and looked sillier, particularly when trying to solve the simple mystery of the visitors' attack.

Early in the game Clint recognized the sharp difference in the line play of the opposing squads, the all-important factor that can make a team look good even without real talent in the backfield. The timing of the linemen, reduced to seconds or to inches, made all the difference in the world. The proper use of leverage at the proper time was something the Castoffs were learning, but which the Rebels had yet to learn.

Now that Dutch Schwartz, the only student player to make the grade, was playing with the varisty, Clint had no one he could depend on to open holes when they were needed and to plug them when it was required.

Clint, in the role of quarterback, did his best to spot weaknesses in the other team. There were, he knew, plenty of them, but his inexperience failed to draw a picture for him, a prompt, clear picture he could use without delay. The Castoffs, on the other hand, had their coach to spot the Rebels weaknesses, of which there were a multitude. It was a great advantage for the Castoffs and an equally great handicap to their opponents.

Even so, Clint gradually became aware that something very exciting had happened to himself, though his pleasure was dimmed by his inability to make full use of his discovery. Scrimmage sessions had gone far to assure him that his own football ability had improved tremendously. It required an actual game, however, to make him absolutely sure, to confirm his belief that added weight and more exact coordination could bring about the transformation he had hoped for.

Now he knew this change had really come about. He could feel it strongly. His speed was good. Better still, he could control a shifty style of running with a certainty very far removed from his uncertain performance a year ago. He handled the ball with confidence, knowing exactly what he wanted to do with it. He made mistakes, of course, but they came from inexperience instead of clumsiness.

It was frustrating not to be able to use his new ability to advantage. The situation clearly demonstrated the old football adage that a backfield is no better than its line, and a runner no better than his blocking. Yet Clint could not blame his teammates. They were trying desperately but futilely, because they were not yet securely grounded in the simple fundamentals of the game.

The Rebels' only chance to advance the ball, Clint soon found out, was through the air. He fooled the Castoffs with a long touchdown pass to Yancy, for the Rebels' only score. Repeated passing encountered the expected road block. The Castoffs, taking advantage of their superior line play, began to outwit Clint by opening a hole to permit a backfield defensive man to shoot the gap, charging into the Rebel backfield to clobber Clint before he had a chance to get the pass away.

The game settled down to a pattern—a gruesome pattern for the Rebels. The men had courage. They gave everything they had, squandering their energy in a hopeless cause. Clint used his replacements as well as his experience would permit, but what he was able to do did not help much.

The fans enjoyed the game—the early part of it, at least. Most of them were there to ridicule the unpredictable antics of the opposing teams, and they found plenty to amuse them.

When the score began to mount in favor of the visitors, however, the merriment began to fade. Laughter and wisecracks were replaced by a definite annoyance tinged strongly with embarrassment. The Rebels, after all, were the home team. They were taking a disgraceful beating which was no longer funny.

Another blow fell during the final period of the game. The Rebel left guard, Bob Creel, lay writhing on the ground when they unearthed him from the bottom of a line play, his leg broken. He was carried from the field and sent promptly to the hospital.

The game continued under a cloud. The fans, fed up with the poor showing of the Rebels, began to straggle off in disgust. There were not many left when the final score was posted: Castoffs 42, Rebels 6.

A disheartened squad of Rebels returned to the dressing room. Clint felt he ought to try to cheer them up, but he soon gave up the thought. What could he say to a group of bruised and battered men who had seen a bright dream go up in smoke? Could he tell them there were better days ahead? Why lie to them? They undoubtedly knew what lay ahead.

CHAPTER
11

Immediate developments following the catastrophe were more or less predictable, but Clint, even though he had braced himself for the repercussions, was dropped into an even deeper pit of gloom. In his column, Max Hacker hopped eagerly on the Rebels' defeat like a robin jumping on a worm. It was a happy vindication of his previous predictions.

"What else could we expect?" he crowed. "It was in the books right from the start. A football team without authoritative leadership is like a ship without a rudder—going nowhere.

"We have no quarrel, as we have said in the past, with anyone who wants to sail a boat like that on his own private pond, but when he tries to match his contraption against properly steered boats we think it's time to call a halt.

"Why should these men who call themselves the Rebels be forced to humiliate themselves by a pitiful performance such as they staged yesterday? More pointedly, why should they be permitted to humiliate their school which, reluctantly, finds itself associated with this rabble called a football team?

"And finally," he pointed out with a touch of glee, "may I refresh your memory as to my prediction that this team was laying itself wide open to serious injuries. Well, it happened yesterday. And who can guess how many more poor kids will suffer the same fate under incompetent leadership and coaching?"

"The stinker!" Yancy growled, when he had read the column.

"Yeah," agreed Clint morosely. "I guess that's what he is. And the worst of it is, he's mostly right. I've made a mess of things."

"Why blame yourself?"

"Who else can I blame?" Clint demanded.

"Quick kicking yourself around," said Yancy gruffly. "Maybe we learned something in that game. We'll do better in the game next Friday."

"That's as good a hope as any," Clint said, without enthusiasm.

When the Rebels reported for the Monday practice session Clint did his best to restore their spirits, but it was like trying to start a fire with soggy fuel. Some of the men made an effort to respond. The majority were listless, almost sullen, with the air of disillusioned men who had been badly cheated.

The dedicated band of hecklers picked this time to come up with a new wrinkle. For their purpose the moment was well chosen. They caught the Rebels in an ugly mood, with their resistance at low ebb, ripe for some sort of action to bolster their discouragement and not caring much what might result from such an action.

The halfhearted workout was under way when the howling of a siren drew attention to an ambulance coming toward the field. The siren growled to silence as the vehicle pulled up near the side line.

It was not a standard ambulance, but the illusion was well concocted. A station wagon had been rigged up with the word *Ambulance* painted on each side. Completing the picture were a pair of coeds dressed as nurses and a pair of students representing interns in white suits with stethoscopes dangling from their necks. The "interns," moving in a businesslike manner, lowered the tailgate, removed a stretcher, and placed it on the ground. They then stood about with an expectant air, awaiting their first customer.

It was a good show, even though the performance

was a bit on the sinister side. The fans, on hand to watch the workout, began to enjoy it. Amused smiles appeared on their faces. More significantly, they began to watch the Rebels with curious interest, wondering how Clint would meet the situation.

Clint was wondering the same thing himself. The Rebels, seeing nothing funny in the gag, began to heat up. They had suspended all activity and were shooting ominous glances in the direction of the wagon. They were burning on a short fuse today, and Clint shuddered inwardly at the thought that all his previous warnings to the men could easily be forgotten at this moment. The Rebels were in a reckless mood.

Clint forced himself to think with every ounce of brains he had. His thoughts, sluggish at first, began to form a hopeful pattern. "Hold it!" he told the men, a note of desperation in his voice. "Hold it, will you? I think I'm having a brainstorm."

They obeyed him grudgingly, willing to give him a chance before taking matters into their own hands. Clint's thought took form, blossoming suddenly into an inspiration.

"I think I've got it," he announced. "Come close and listen hard." When they formed a group about him, he said, "First I want you guys to keep looking just as sore as you are. Let's not tip 'em off. Keep scowling."

Clint hastily outlined his plan, and the Rebels

liked it. They found it hard to keep scowling. A few delighted snorts could be heard.

"I think Yancy can pull it off as well as anyone, because he's the biggest ham," said Clint. "What do you think?"

They all signified their approval.

Yancy said in a choked voice, "I—I'm deeply touched. And I won't let you down, dear friends."

The Rebels went on with the scrimmage. A few minutes later Yancy unobtrusively loosened the laces of his right shoe. On the next play he remained upon the ground, twitching convulsively with pain. His teammates gathered around him in concern, giving Yancy a chance to slip the shoe partially off his foot, leaving it twisted at a convincingly ugly angle.

"It's busted!" came Yancy's agonized cry, loud enough for the alarmed fans to hear.

Clint started jogging toward the ambulance. "Hey you guys!" he yelled. "Bring that stretcher out here on the double!"

The men in the white suits began to panic. They both grabbed at the stretcher, with the obvious intention of getting it back into the ambulance with all possible speed. They both grabbed the same end of the stretcher, battling for possession. Clint reached them before they made much progress.

"Get that stretcher on the field!" he ordered.

The interns were as white as their uniforms now.

One of them found strength to stutter, "B-b-but we're not doctors!"

"Then what are you doing in those outfits?"

"We—we just thought—"

"Congratulations," Clint cut in. "I didn't know jerks like you *could* think." Then he turned to a couple of husky Rebels who had joined. "I'll bring Yancy back to the wagon while you boys stay here and see that the doctors don't go anywhere."

Clint hurried back on the field with the stretcher. Yancy was placed tenderly upon it. Clint and another Rebel lifted the stretcher carefully and started for the side line. When they drew near the station wagon, Yancy was groaning pitifully and as they arrived he forced words through his clenched teeth.

"The bones! They're grinding together! I can feel 'em. A-a-a-h!"

"Put him in the wagon," ordered Clint. "These punks'll take him to the hospital."

With a final show of courage, one of the interns blocked the way. "No, no, you can't!" he squeaked. "We can't take him to the hospital in *this!* We'd get in lots of trouble. We'd—"

"You're already in lots of trouble," Clint told him harshly. "You've faked an ambulance and you're posing as doctors—and nurses," he added, as an afterthought, gesturing at the women huddled like scared rabbits in the front seat of the car. "Now what'll it be? Are you going to take this man to the hospital?"

While the scared men were trying to make up their minds Yancy timed his next move nicely. With a flip of his right foot he sent the shoe flying through the air.

"Nuts!" he said disgustedly. "I can't wait all day."

With this assertion he climbed off the stretcher. He tested his right ankle, jumping up and down on it. "Seems O.K.," he said. Then he explained, with a grin, to the startled fans who had gathered at the spot. "I heal fast."

The shocked silence last several moments, broken finally when the fans realized what had happened. The grins turned into snickers and the snickers turned into belly laughs. The gagsters, tumbling to the fact that they had been out-gagged, regained their color—lots of color. They were bright with humiliation as they climbed into their ambulance for an undignified departure. The siren, as they left the field, was silent.

The Rebels' morale was slightly higher when the practice session was resumed. They had weathered another crisis and had come out top dog. The satisfaction of the moment temporarily dulled their other worries.

It was a short reprieve, however. Despite all

Clint's and Yancy's efforts during the next few days, the Rebels slumped once more into their discouraged frame of mind. Some abandoned all pretense and quit the squad, making no bones about the fact that they had had enough—they had been played for suckers and had learned their lesson.

Clint could not blame them much. He blamed them even less when the Rebels took another thrashing in their second game. They played like men who did not care what happened. When the game was over they slunk off the field. The score was 36-0.

Max Hacker had another field day. He loaded up and took pot shots at everything in sight. Clint, reading about his colossal failure, was almost frightened by his lack of interest. He felt as his men must have felt when they went down to defeat the second time—he did not care what happened now. It was a dangerous mood and he did not dare to coddle it.

"It's not the end of the world," said Yancy, feebly optimistic.

"No," conceded Clint. "It's just the end of the Rebels. I bit off more than I could chew. I started something I can't finish. That's what hurts."

"How do you know we're finished?"

"Just a hunch, and a big one. Grant's called another meeting in his office Monday. We may get orders from the top to call the whole thing off."

Yancy winced. "Not good. Not good at all."

Clint slapped a hand on the arm of his chair. "If we only had a coach!" he exploded irritably. "But I guess it's too late now," he finished gloomily.

The paper containing Max Hacker's latest blast was still on Clint's knees. He started to brush it angrily to the floor when a news story on the same page caught his eye. It was headlined in large type, making him wonder why he had not seen it sooner. He grabbed the paper and began to stiffen as his eyes raced through the story.

Yancy, watching him, demanded, "What goes on?"

Clint handed the paper to Yancy, indicating the headlines: "Shag Conway Injured—Lost to Vulcans for Season." Yancy read it with a puzzled frown, then drew his breath in sharply. "Hey!" he exclaimed hoarsely. "Do you think he *would?*"

"Who knows? But I'm sure it's worth the chance. It says in the paper it was a simple fracture and that he was able to go home after they put on the cast." Clint glanced at his watch. "Seven-thirty. He ought to be at his house now. I'm going over."

"Good luck," said Yancy fervently. "You'll need it."

Clint walked the short distance to Shag Conway's fraternity house, bolstering his shaky confidence as he went along. He knew Shag only by reputation, as a national football figure and a powerhouse in the Vulcan backfield. He had heard no rumors indicating that Shag was anything but a nice guy who had borne his fame as well as could be expected. There was a vast gap, however, between a man of Shag's caliber and a sophomore such as Clint. Clint knew his present mission was presumptuous, that nothing but desperation could have forced him to attempt the thing he was about to try. He rang the doorbell and a freshman answered it.

"I want to talk to Shag Conway," Clint announced.

"Well," the freshman said uncertainly, "he's in his room, but. . . . Well, I'll see." He moved to the foot of the stairs and yelled, "Hey Shag, there's a guy down here to see you."

"Send him up."

"O.K. Third door on the left," the freshman instructed Clint.

The door was open. Shag was studying beneath a desk lamp which threw the rest of the room in shadow. He was big, towheaded, and homely. His left arm was in a sling. Clint had seen him on the campus, but at close range he looked more formidable.

"Well?" he inquired, as Clint stood in the doorway.

Clint swallowed against the dryness in his throat, then said inanely, "I—I'm sorry about your arm."

"Yeah, tough," Shag grunted. "What's on your mind?"

Clint took a couple of tentative steps into the room. "My name's Clint Martin," he said, introducing himself.

Shag moved the light with his good hand, expelling the shadows. He took a good look at Clint before saying, "Yeah, I've heard of you. Sit down."

Clint eased himself uncomfortably into a chair. Shag studied him further before observing, "You don't look like the sort of guy who could raise so much stink around this school."

"I didn't mean to," said Clint, still apologizing. "After I got the thing started I found I was in over my head."

"You can say *that* again," said Shag. Then he asked curiously, "What happened?"

Clint shrugged. "I was stupid," he admitted. "I should have known it would develop into something bigger than I planned on. I should have had brains enough to start at the beginning—and find someone who would agree to coach us."

Shag's smile was thin but not unpleasant. "From what I hear you sure need a coach."

Clint sneaked a deep breath into his lungs before jumping in with both feet. "I'm here to ask you to take on the job."

A surprised jerk brought a grunt of pain from Shag. He eased his arm into a more comfortable position, then burst out, "Are you nuts? To ask *me* to mess around with a bunch of clowns who don't know their left feet from their right?"

He glared at Clint in outrage. Clint met the glare with narrowed eyes as his anger rose. There was no humbleness in his apology this time. "Sorry—I must have forgotten who you were."

An odd look replaced the indignation in Shag's eyes. Instead of staging the explosion Clint was braced for, Shag leaned back in his chair and rubbed a big hand across his face, the gesture of a man trying to bring his thoughts in line. After a moment Shag said, as if talking to himself, "I must have forgotten too."

Clint realized that this was not the moment for further comment, so he kept his mouth shut, watching with interest while Shag organized his thoughts.

When Shag spoke his voice was mildly sheepish. "You caught me at a bad time, Clint. I've been feeling sorry for myself, and when a guy feels sorry for himself it can throw a lot of things out of gear, such as making him think he's a bigger wheel than he really is. Do you follow me?"

"I think I do. You've had a hard kick in the teeth."

"Not hard enough," Shag said irritably, "to make me go off half-cocked the way I did. Just because I've got enough natural talent to be an all-American doesn't give me the right to run down men like yourself who want to play football and are willing to make sacrifices to do it. What sort of material have you got?"

Shag's quick reversal caught Clint by surprise. He tried to subdue his swift elation, knowing that nothing definite was settled.

"Well," he told Shag with a grin, "we *do* know the difference between our right and left feet, but we don't know what to do about it. When I tell you about our material you must understand it's my own personal opinion, and that I don't know too much about it, to start with."

"Give it a whirl, anyway."

"Frankly," Clint went on, "I think we have real possibilities. The men who are most likely to stick around are those who went through the cram session for the freshmen students. They didn't learn much, but they proved they had guts. I think we're all fairly well based in fundamentals, which means we're conditioned to learn other things without too much waste of time. Our big weakness is team play. We need to be coordinated."

Shag leaned back in his chair to mull it over. Clint gave him all the time he needed. Shag said at last, "Well, I'll take a stab at it. I'm not an experienced coach, but I know football and someday I want to be a coach. I might as well start now. Besides, it'll keep me from feeling sorry for myself."

Clint's elation at this point was almost too great to subdue. He checked himself, however. "We're not out of the woods yet," he confessed. "There'll be a powwow with Mr. Grant tomorrow morning. Crawford may have decided to wipe out the whole deal."

"As bad as that?"

"It might not be that bad now. Your agreeing to help us might swing a lot of weight. And that brings up another point. What effect will it have on your relations with the Athletic Department?"

"I've thought about that," Shag said, grinning. "Herb Crawford will probably want to shoot me for a traitor. It's no secret around the place that he'd like to see this deal of yours fold up, so he could say I told you so."

"And?"

Shag shrugged his shoulders. "Herb's not a bad guy. I like him. On the other hand, I don't owe him anything. I've more than earned my pay. I won't play any more football until I turn pro, so if I coach you guys it's nobody's business but my own. I honestly like the idea of this thing you've started and I'd hate to see it fold."

"So you'll help us?"

"It's a deal."

CHAPTER
12

Clint was feeling a lot better when he left Shag's room. The situation was still touch and go, but he believed now that he had some reliable ammunition to bolster his position. He could go to the Monday meeting armed with something more formidable than a pea shooter. He was quivering inside, nevertheless, when he reported at Grant's office, joining the gloomy conclave of Grant, Maggie Parnell, and Grady Bell.

"It looks like curtains, boys," said Maggie sadly. "Mr. Crawford's had enough. He claims you've had a fair chance. He feels that the school can no longer be subjected, and I quote, 'to the disgraceful performances which reflect upon Midwestern's athletic standards.' That's the verdict, gentlemen. I'm afraid we're licked—unless someone can pull an elephant out of a hat."

"Maybe I can," Clint offered quietly.

It was an attention-grabbing statement. Clint held the center of the floor while they stared at him with cautious hope. When he told them about Shag Conway, a gleam of hope flickered in the others' eyes.

"Is that straight?" demanded Grady.

"It's straight," Clint assured him.

"Hum-m-m," mused Grant. His eyes swung toward Maggie Parnell. "Well?" he demanded pointedly.

Maggie Parnell was not one to be railroaded into a snap judgment. She gave the matter proper thought before saying, "It's just possible we might get a reversed decision. My best lever, of course, will be the merchants who have backed the Rebels. I honestly believe the boss would like to give them a reasonable run for their money, and with Shag Conway in the picture, he might make some sort of concession."

"How soon can you find out?" asked Grant.

"He's in a good mood this morning and not too busy. This should be as logical a time as any. Keep your fingers crossed."

She left the office. Grady got up and paced the floor. Grant sweated it out by drawing doodles on a desk pad. Clint sat and suffered, his raw nerves playing tricks. There was an electric clock on the wall and he watched the seconds pass. He also watched the door, and when Maggie finally entered he drew his breath in sharply. She had the grim look of a person who has just weathered a tough fight.

She did not take advantage of her chance to prolong the suspense. "A reprieve," she told them promptly. "It's the best I could do. The execution is delayed."

"How long?" Clint demanded.

Maggie shrugged. "It all depends. He was not happy about Shag's part in it, which was to be expected, so he's swinging a haymaker at Shag too. The Rebels will win their next two games—or else. That's it, boys."

"Two games?" asked Grant. "Why two?"

"It figures," Maggie said. "Two games would make it a decisive test. There's always the possibility that the Rebels might win the first one by luck."

"Ha!" exploded Grady. "Fat chance!"

"Giving up?" demanded Maggie.

"Just about," admitted Grady. "Because I happen to know something you don't. The Stafford University team, which calls itself the Orphans, will be loaded. A couple of varsity men were dropped from the squad for low grades. They're playing with the Orphans to keep in shape until they can boost their grades."

"That could be rough," conceded Grant. "But why hang out the crepe until we have to? We're still alive. That's all that matters now. How about it, Clint?"

Clint nodded. "We have an open date next Friday. That gives us a couple of weeks to get ready for the game. It could be a whole lot worse." He turned to Grant. "I'd better tell Shag what he's up against. May I use your phone?"

"Help yourself. But he's probably in class right now."

"I'll take a chance."

The chance paid off. Shag was called to the phone at the fraternity house. Clint explained briefly what had happened at the meeting.

Shag decided promptly. "They're long odds, Clint, but I like 'em that way. See you at the field this afternoon. I may be a little late."

Clint still clung to his slender thread of optimism when he started for the field. It suffered a severe strain when he arrived. The few men already there were grim, as if on hand through habit rather than through a desire to play more football. These were the rugged ones, the ones who found it hard to quit. Clint withheld his news, preferring to find out how many more would come.

They straggled in, all in the same tight-lipped mood. Some of them tried feeble jokes, abandoning the effort when the jokes flopped over on their backs and died. Others refused to look at Clint, not wanting him to see the accusation in their eyes.

Clint weathered a bad moment when it was evident no more Rebels would show up. There were not enough to fill the uniforms provided by the businesses. The squad had withered to a skeleton. The men were irritable and touchy.

"What are you smirking about, Yancy?" one of them complained. "Do you know something we don't know?"

"Yes," said Clint, "he does. I wanted to wait until you were all here before telling you we've got a coach—Shag Conway. He ought to be here soon."

Somebody snarled, "Don't kid us, mister!"

"It's on the level," Clint assured him.

The atmosphere of the room changed like magic. Once recovered from the jolt, the men began to speculate excitedly. There was no more listless donning of equipment. A shoestring tied with too much force popped audibly.

Clint braced himself for his next announcement. "That was the good news," he told them. "Here's the bad. Crawford has handed down an ultimatum. If we don't win our next two games, he'll wipe us out. That's how it stands."

Determined not to let the Rebels' hopes soar out of reach, he told them of the two varsity men who would play on the Orphan squad, yet even this announcement failed to change a condition that Clint found slightly frightening. The Rebels took the news too casually, discounting its importance. Their unspoken attitude was, "Nuts to Crawford! Nuts to the Orphans! So we'll win!"

Seeking an explanation for their attitude, Clint found it by recalling what these men had been through. They were mostly those who had weathered the freshman student ordeal, defying the organized attempt to discourage them. They were men who had taken two sound thrashings in two weeks, yet who were now reporting for more football, with its prospect of more thrashings. They were men who loved the game of football, men who needed no more than a spark of encouragement to make them believe that they could win. They were blandly refusing now to acknowledge the tremendous odds against them. Poor blind fools, thought Clint, knowing his sympathy was wasted.

Shag Conway worked with the remaining men for several days before submitting a cautious diagnosis. "It's too early to be sure, Clint," he said, "because I'm still feeling my way along as a coach. We're certainly not overloaded with talent, but we've definitely got something to use as a substitute—the willingness of these men to work and learn, for what it may be worth to us. These guys love football."

There was another element Shag failed to mention. The Rebels, since they had been organized, had had no one to pin their faith to. They had recognized their coaching as haphazard and lacking sufficient knowledge or experience to make them believe that they were learning what they should. They had, as a result, been too uncertain of the things they were supposed to do.

With Shag as boss, the setup was entirely different. The Rebels believed in Shag. Convinced that he knew his football, they were willing to accept his word as gospel, and to soak up, without reservation, all he taught them.

Another factor worked strongly in Shag's favor. Aware of his limitations as a coach, he had sense enough to move with care. Instead of grabbing the reins with a rough hand, he let his reputation serve as his authority. Feeling his way like this brought him closer to the men, because it made it possible for him to receive willing obedience.

So the Rebels toiled and sweated, a dedicated crew. When word got out that Shag was in command, a few of the deserters came back, reporting with a hang-dog air, but they soon felt the new spirit Shag's leadership brought. Soon they had settled down and were working as hard as the rest. The billboard uniforms were all in use again.

Most of the fans had lost interest in the Rebels. An

occasional few, however, showed up to watch the workouts, but they wore the indifferent air of people who had nothing better to occupy their time. One of the regulars was Shoo-fly Finnigan, whose persistence surprised Clint.

After a noisy arrival on the scooter he would sit quietly throughout the workout, watching the activity on the field without expression. It failed to make much sense to Clint, in view of Shoo-fly's loud contention that football was a stupid game for stupid people. His close attention to the game these days seemed to belie the statement.

Clint, hoping to satisfy his own curiosity, had approached Shoo-fly several times, intending to explain things Shoo-fly might not understand. Each time Clint had been rebuffed. Shoo-fly merely grunted. He obviously intended to make no statement that might incriminate him.

One day, however, the information popped out—in the true sense of the phrase. When Shoo-fly was ready to leave he always woke the echoes of the stadium with the snorting blast of his scooter, letting in the clutch with a force that always snapped his head back. This time his derby was almost dislodged. He made an involuntary grab for it, forcing him to take one hand off the handle bars, a tactical blunder which made the machine swerve toward a rough spot near the edge of the field. When the front wheel hit the bumps a lot of things began to happen all at once, with Shoo-fly in the middle of the stage.

The scooter began bucking like an enraged bull. A rodeo champ would surely have been dumped, but Shoo-fly, a champ in his own right, stuck doggedly to his mount. There was daylight between him and the saddle several times, but skill and luck brought him down each time for another bounce into the air.

It was during one of these big bounces that Shoo-fly hit the saddle a bit off center, and a small book popped from the side pocket of his coat. Clint was hurrying to the spot in alarm, hoping to catch the old man on the fly, when he finally bounced too high to regain his seat on the scooter.

Clint's efforts were wasted. Shoo-fly, as a last resort, reverted to his horse-and-buggy days. "Whoa!" he bellowed. "Whoa, you blasted beast!"

It appeared to be the magic word. The scooter gave a feeble buck, coughed hoarsely, and subsided. Shoo-fly, still the master, sat defiantly and glared about him, daring anyone to laugh.

"Are you all right, Mr. Finnigan?" asked Clint.

"What do you mean, am I all right!" roared Shoo-fly. "Do I look sick, or something?"

Clint, having learned the hard way that he had chosen the wrong subject, hastened to undo the error, but he only managed to get himself in still more trouble. He retrieved the small book and brought it back to Shoo-fly, noticing too late that he was holding an official football guide. "You—you dropped this, sir," he stammered.

Shoo-fly's look of outraged shock could not have been more genuine if someone had caught him with a set of burglar's tools. His disgraceful secret was revealed. He was a trapped man, stamped with the brand of guilt. He snatched the book and jammed it into his pocket, too shamed for anger.

Regaining a measure of composure, he said to Clint, "And now I'm sure of it. Any game that has to be controlled by all the double talk right here in this book is a stupid game."

His eyes challenged Clint to deny it. Clint said, "Yes, sir," trying hard to keep his face straight. When the effort became too great, he turned back toward the field. As he returned to the squad he grinned. "The grand old fraud," he muttered half aloud.

The days ahead were crowded. Shag worked the Rebels hard; he was a tough boss but a fair one, and there were no complaints. As order gradually replaced confusion in the squad, a few things came into clearer focus. The Rebels, as Shag had pointed out, were not loaded with talent; yet, working with their new-found unity, they showed signs of promise. It looked that way, at least, in scrimmage. How they would look against tougher competition was anybody's guess, and Clint tried hard not to guess.

There were no scouting reports on the Orphans. However, the yardstick by which the Rebels had to measure was accurate enough to be alarming. Aided by their two varsity men, the Orphans were undefeated in two games. They had licked the Castoffs, the first team that had overrun the Rebels. The Rebels, of course, had improved. How much they had improved was still a big question.

A positive factor on the optimistic side was the development of Shag Conway as a coach. Clint, though his experience with football coaches was definitely limited, could not help but feel that Shag possessed the necessary qualities. He seemed to have the touch. He was a tireless worker, patient or strict as the occasion required. He was a good analyst, quick to spot a fundamental improvement that would do the most for a player's game. He formed the players into small groups for intensive training, hammering home a single point until they learned it. He held skull sessions, not for the purpose of diagramming plays, but to instill the value and the common sense of basic football strategy.

As for the plays themselves, Shag showed commendable restraint. He did not succumb to the inclination of a new coach to present the world with something new and different, just to show what a clever guy he was. He stuck to simple standard plays.

"We haven't time," he told the Rebels, "to learn fancy stuff. If I tried to cram you with a lot of razzle-dazzle it might only foul things up. Even the trickiest play isn't worth the chalk it takes to put it on the blackboard if the play isn't pulled off to perfection. On the other hand, the ordinary bread-and-butter plays are always dangerous, and they'll click ninety percent of the time if every man does exactly what he is supposed to do. That's why I'm limiting the squad to a bare minimum of plays. If you learn them, and learn them right, you'll always know what you're doing. There won't be any guesswork. That's important."

The time passed much too swiftly. With the Orphan game almost upon them, Clint was not at all sure that the men were ready. He was not sure that he himself was ready despite the definite improvements in his game that he had noticed under Shag's intensive training. His ball handling behind the line was smoother, more deceptive, his passing pattern more exact, yet he knew he still had lots to learn.

Before the game Shag delivered a few frank remarks. "Those uniforms of yours are a sight," he said. "I'd be ashamed to send you in a game with them. The Orphans may or may not pin our ears back, but if they think they're playing against a bunch of hoboes, it'll boost their confidence. And it will boost the morale of you guys if you go out there looking clean. So have those outfits cleaned. You won't need them on the day before the game, because you're only getting a light workout. If you're pressed for dough I'll loan it to you."

"Coach," said Yancy soberly, "maybe you're overlooking a good bet. If we go into the game with this fine, healthy odor the other guys might think we're billy goats. It'd make 'em careless."

"I'm posing as a coach," Shag said with a grin, "so I've got to have my principles. I couldn't bring myself to take such low-down advantage of another team."

CHAPTER
13

Clint's nerves were in bad shape the night before the game. Yancy, no better off, suggested that a movie might help them. Clint, exerting considerable will power, decided to stay home and do some necessary studying, so Yancy went to the movie by himself.

Clint tackled his books, only to find that his will power was not as strong as he had believed. The words he read would not sink in. They made no sense. Instead, dim outlines of football diagrams seemed, in some way, to find their way upon the pages.

He finally gave up the effort as hopeless, allowing his mind to grapple with the crowding thoughts which could not be kept out. He had to face the frightening fact that the responsibility would be largely his in the game against the Orphans. He was the one who would have to run the team. Despite the help he would receive from Shag, many of the decisions would have to be his own. It would be so easy to guess wrong at times, particularly with his limited experience. He would hold the future of the Rebels in his hands. He shoved his chair back violently from the table and ran a sleeve across his perspiring forehead.

Then he began to pace the room, only to find the space too limited to relieve his tension. Finally he left the dormitory and began to walk, scarcely aware that his steps had led him to the Rebels' stadium. He sat in the bleachers, trying to absorb the calm of the still night.

His nerves began to unwind slowly. The familiar surroundings may have helped, even though he sensed them rather than saw them, in the darkness. His imagination was an ally, centering his thoughts upon the fact that other men had fought their battles on this field, battles against uncertainty and fear. He was not the only man to face a crisis on the gridiron. Men had done it in the past and would do so in the future—a conviction that went far toward making him feel less alone.

When the quiet of the stadium, peopled with old ghosts, had done its job, Clint got up to leave. He was slightly ashamed now of the emotions he had carried there, but he was grateful that he could leave them there. He was feeling a lot better when he started home.

The Rebels reported for the game in bright clean uniforms. They went through a little horseplay in displaying them, but beneath their antics was a dangerous tautness, as if they were facing for the first time the tremendous importance of this game. Clint knew how the men were feeling. Despite a restful night his apprehensions had returned.

Shag recognized the symptoms. "This is the toughest part," he told them, "so sweat it out. I can't help you much right now. That, I hope, will come later, when I see both teams in action. I'll be up in the stands with a field phone and a pair of binoculars. There will always be someone at the other end of the phone on the bench. I'll send in advice with the replacements."

Referring to the Orphans' two varsity men, Clint asked, "Any more dope on Carl Britt and Stan Flack?"

"Only what I've told you," replied Shag. "Britt's the power runner, Flack's the end. Maybe I can come up with something when I see Britt in action. As for Flack, the only thing we can do at the start is to try to keep him covered with our two fastest backfield men, Tom Archer and Clint. You've already been assigned that job. It will weaken our pass defense, but we've got to take the chance. Any more questions?"

There were a few—merely nervous inquiries of no great importance. Shag, however, gave them serious consideration before answering. When he finally sent the Rebels to the field, they kept closely bunched on the way as if trying to absorb confidence from one another.

Things were better when they reached the field, spread out, and began their warm-up. The feel of the ball and the tonic of action relieved them of some tension. The sight of the Orphans, also warming up, helped too. They looked less formidable than the Rebels had pictured them in their imagination. They were just another bunch of guys in billboard uniforms, who neither ran their signals, passed, nor kicked any better than the Rebels.

Clint was surprised at the number of fans who showed up for the game. Many of them were probably merely curious—ready to leave when things got dull. The others might have come there in the hope of seeing the Rebels play a more acceptable game of football under the coaching of Shag Conway. Beyond that point Clint gave the matter little thought. He had other things to think about.

Clint, as captain of the Rebels, met the opposing captain, Griff Ricker, in the center of the field for the coin toss. Ricker, also a quarterback, was a well-built, good-looking kid.

Shaking hands, he grinned and said, "I'm sure glad to meet you, Clint. You had a terrific idea when you started this league, and a lot of us are grateful to you."

"Thanks," said Clint. "I hope we can keep it rolling."

"So do I. Good luck today."

"The same to you."

The referee tossed the coin. Ricker called heads. It came up tails. The referee turned to Clint.

"We'll kick," said Clint.

He caught the surprised, slightly wary look in Ricker's eyes. Ricker was wondering if the Rebels had been underestimated, if their faith in their defense would permit a ground-gaining team, such as the Orphans, to get first hands upon the ball. The theory in this instance was that the Rebels would hold for downs, forcing a kick deep in Orphan territory.

The theory, confusing as it was to Ricker, had not influenced Clint's choice. He had acted on instructions from Shag Conway.

"Kick if you get the chance," the coach had told him. "Defensive action will give the boys a chance to settle down. They won't be quite so jumpy when they have to handle the ball, and there'll be less chance of fumbling in our own end of the field. I've got another reason, too. I may be taking a chance, but I want to get a look at their offense as soon as possible. If I can spot anything important it might pay off later in the game."

The Orphans deployed to receive the kick. While Clint was teeing up the ball on his own forty-yard line he was planning a little early strategy. He noticed that Carl Britt occupied the place of honor, the deep center spot in front of the goal posts.

He was not a tall man. His weight had moved sideways instead of up. He was built along the general lines of a small tank, suggesting that his speed was limited. Clint reasoned, though, that Britt must be faster than he looked, otherwise he would not be occupying the position of the man most likely to receive the kickoff.

In a situation of this sort, Clint decided, smart tactics called for an off-center kick to keep the ball away from Britt. When the whistle blew, he made his short run and banged his toe against the ball, aiming for the left-hand corner of the field.

It was his first error in judgment. Clint was a reasonably good kicker, but not good enough as yet to call his shots. The ball headed to the left, all right, but too far to the left. It went out-of-bounds on the fifteen-yard line, giving the Rebels their first bad break of the game.

Clint tried not to act as guilty as he felt while the referee was bringing the ball back to the thirty-five yard line for another kickoff. He noted uneasily that the Rebels seemed a trifle shaken by the incident, but consoled himself with the hope that this brief relaxation from tension might serve to steady them a bit.

On his second effort he gave up all foolish notions of trying to be smart. He put all his beef into the kick, getting off a pretty good one down the center. Carl Britt, as Clint had feared, hauled in the kick on the fifteen-yard line and started up the field.

Britt's opening burst of speed was startling. His short, huge legs carried him across the ground like a water bug skittering across a pond. He made no attempt to swerve as the Rebels closed in on him; he just kept on coming like a small tornado.

An Orphan threw a block at Clint, which was only partially effective. Momentarily staggered, Clint regained his balance in time to get a reaching hand on Britt. He felt as if he had tried to grab a two-hundred-pound bowling ball. It could not have been called a tackle, but it slowed Britt down enough to permit the other Rebels to pile over him on the thirty-four-yard line.

Clint shut his mind to the excitement of the moment, forcing himself to evaluate what he had seen and learned. He lay on the ground a moment, giving his impressions a brief chance to drop into their proper slots.

His first conviction was that Britt's gain would have been considerably longer behind better blocking. Maybe the Orphans had been overeager or overconfident, but Clint's optimistic guess was that the Orphans, as a team, were no more talent-laden than the Rebels. He figured that the difference in the two teams would have to be measured in terms of Britt and Flack—a difference, he was reluctant to admit, which could be serious.

Another conclusion also had to do with Britt. He was not a halfback, with sustained speed. His early burst of speed, though alarming, had not increased once he was under way. He was not particularly shifty. He was merely a human battering ram, yet the threat this presented could not be overlooked. A man like Britt was valuable to any squad during the numerous times when short yardage was needed for a first down.

Clint, calling the defensive signals, used his best judgment. It seemed logical to him that the Orphans, in their own territory, would test the Rebel line with their formidable ground weapon, Britt, a probing tactic to gather information. Clint, therefore, warned the Rebels of a line plunge.

It looked for an instant as if Clint's guess was right. From his deep linebacking spot he saw—or thought he saw—Griff Ricker jam the ball into Britt's belly. Clint had taken a few swift steps toward the line of scrimmage when, with an alarmed grunt, he saw Ricker fading back to pass behind good protection. The Rebels had been expecting a line play.

Clint plowed to a halt. Fighting off a stab of panic, he did the instinctive thing, swerving toward his left to cover the right end, Stan Flack. The instinct was sound enough but much too late. Flack, moving with smooth, rangy speed, was in the clear.

Flack's speed was diminished, however, by repeated glances across his shoulder. The significance of this did not hit Clint right away, even when Flack was justified in his precaution. The pass was short and somewhat wobbly; otherwise, it would have been a touchdown pass.

It obviously was not intended for a buttonhook, yet Flack was forced to play it in that way. He whirled and backtracked with a coordination beautiful to watch. No one but a great receiver could have made that catch. Flack made it with a dive, a long reach, and a pair of powerful hands. He was on the ground for a twenty-two yard gain when Clint arrived.

Clint stood for a thoughtful moment, tucking away another bit of information. There was little doubt as to Flack's greatness as a pass receiver, but there was considerable doubt as to Griff Ricker's ability as a passer. Knowing this, Flack had had to keep his eye upon the ball, rather than run directly to the spot where a well-thrown pass should reach him. It was a tidy bit of knowledge, which Clint hoped would be of use.

When the Orphans went into their huddle, the guessing game was dumped on Clint again. There was no way of telling how badly he had shaken the Rebels' confidence with his first bad guess—he only knew he dared not shake it any further.

Once more he did the best he could. "Loosen the defense," he told them. "Pretend we're expecting another pass, but dig in for a quick move at Britt. I think he's due."

Clint's guessing luck was better this time. Ricker faded a few steps, as if to pass, then fed the ball to Britt on a delayed buck over the left side of the Rebel line; and Clint, from his deep linebacking spot, saw a devastating show of power.

The Rebel line held fairly well, refusing to give Britt much of a hole. It did not seem to make much difference. His solid shoulders battered through what hole there was, forcing it wider with the violence of his charge. Marty Platt, Rebel left tackle, got his arms around Britt's waist. A pair of linebackers also hooked onto Britt. He carried all three of them along, refusing to go down until Clint piled in, his added weight bringing Britt to a halt. It was an eight-yard gain—a frightening gain—leaving the impression with the Rebels that Britt could do it any time he wanted to. As if to prove it, Britt plowed through for five more yards to a first down on the Rebel thirty-one-yard line.

The Rebels were unnerved, bewildered by the Orphan juggernaut with the ability to gain at will. Clint sensed their angry hopelessness. How, they were wondering desperately, could a guy like that be stopped by a team of the Rebels' limited ability? Clint too was wondering. He scrambled for an answer but found none.

A Rebel substitute came rushing in, Randy Keef to replace Paul Dykes at left guard. Clint stared at Keef blankly for an instant, forgetting in the moment of confusion that the responsibility was no longer his. His mind cleared quickly. He snorted with relief. Shag was making his first move. Clint promptly called time out.

The other Rebels' reaction was the same as Clint's. They, too, seemed to have forgotten momentarily that they had a coach. They clustered around Keef like youngsters around a department-store Santa Claus, waiting breathlessly to hear what he would say.

"Shag says," reported Keef, "to quit trying to tackle Britt as if he was a bag of sand. Try to remember he's got a pair of legs and that's where all his power is coming from. As long as he's on his feet he'll be hard to stop, so go in low—submarine him. He doesn't bring his knees up high, which means you might make him trip by falling down in front of him if you can't think of anything better.

"Shag also says to expect a pass on the next play, because they'll probably figure we've doped out some way to slow Britt down, and while we're still concentrating on that they may try to sneak one through the air."

When the referee called time in, the Rebels were breathing easier, more relaxed. It was a big help for them to know that a capable football brain was now on hand to make the big decisions, permitting them to give their whole attention to their individual jobs.

Shag guessed right. A replacement had also come in for the Orphans, probably with that instruction. Ricker faded behind pretty good protection, while Stan Flack sprinted down the side line. Clint and Tom Archer went about their joint assignment to cover Flack. Archer was sticking close to the Orphan man near the side line, but a hunch warned Clint that the pass might not go in that direction, that Flack might cut in toward the center of the field.

Flack did exactly that. Clint closed in on him, watching Flack's eyes and the direction of his swift glances toward the ball. When Flack plowed to a halt and raised his arms to make the catch Clint made his jump between Flack and the coming ball, twisting, as he jumped, for a sight of the ball, hoping for an interception.

Clint saw the ball, all right. He also saw that Flack had made a fool of him. The ball was not coming in the area Flack had reached, it was coming several yards to the right. Clint, still in the air, was helpless to change direction. Flack, well balanced on the ground, had no such problem. A couple of quick steps lined him up with the ball, which settled neatly in his hands. Clint reached the ground in time to whirl, hook an arm around Flack's leg and bring him down, but the damage had been done. Clint also had learned another lesson—watch the ball and never trust a guy like Flack.

The ball went for a twelve-yard gain, bringing the ball to the nineteen-yard line, dangerously deep in Rebel territory. The Orphans opened up on the next play. Ricker moved wide on an option play, faking the pass, then carrying the ball himself for a sweep around the end. He might have gone the distance but for Yancy, who refused to be boxed out. He retained his feet long enough for a lunge, which threw Ricker off balance, permitting Clint to come in for the tackle. Nevertheless, it was a gain of seven yards.

The play had supplied Clint with more information, which was not encouraging. The blocking on the end sweep had been crisp—more efficient than Clint had expected from the Orphans. The sloppy job they had done on the kickoff runback was obviously not a measure of their real ability. They had probably been nervous and overeager at the start of the game. Now that they had settled down, their blocking would be something to contend with. The Orphans had been well coached.

On second down, the Rebels got their first small break of the game, a mix-up in the Orphan backfield. The signals either got fouled up or the ball handling was poor. The Orphans, recovering their own fumble at the line of scrimmage, did not seem concerned over the loss of the down. They had a battering ram to call on.

It was plain from the start of the play that Britt's assignment was to plow out a first down. The Rebels were waiting for him when he made his jet-propelled attack into the line. The Rebel forward wall lunged in with their noses to the ground. Britt's speed was noticeably checked at the line of scrimmage, though he managed, nevertheless, to blast out a hole for himself. Once through it, he was met by the Rebel fullback, Andy Beal, who hurled himself at Britt's shoestrings. Britt toppled forward and was pinned down by Clint and Archer.

The referee spotted the ball and called in the chain. It was as close as that. The chain decided in favor of the Orphans by an inch or so. First down. It was bad news for the Rebels, considerably offset, however, by the satisfying fact that Britt had gained a scant three yards and that the annoyed look on his face advertised his own surprise. To the Rebels, it confirmed the fact that their coach was looking after them. Their awe of Britt was no longer a demoralizing factor.

Ricker sent Britt into the line again, hoping there had been some mistake the last time. The Rebels were not expecting the line plunge as confidently as they had expected the one on the former play, yet the same system of submarining Britt paid off again. He gained four yards this time, a formidable advance but not disastrous. It was satisfying proof, at any rate, that Britt could not tear things apart each time he chose, and that he could be held to moderate gains instead of blasting wide holes any time he wanted to.

The Rebels, pleased with their new discovery, left themselves wide open for a sucker punch. The Orphans lined up for the second down in their usual tight-T. When the ball was snapped, Britt headed, wide open, for the right side of the line. Ricker slapped the ball into Britt's belly, but did not release it. He retained control, concealing the ball behind his leg, then standing innocently to watch the play.

The Rebels fell for it. They converged obediently on Britt, eager as a bunch of show-off kids to display their new technique. Clint, as guilty as any of the others, was pulled in toward the line of scrimmage, discovering too late how badly the Rebels had been foxed.

Griff Ricker, timing the moment nicely, waited until the Rebels had committed themselves before he took off around the end. He had all the blocking anyone could ask for. Brick Ryan, Rebel left end, put up a game but losing battle before he was wiped out.

Clint, belatedly recovering his senses, was nailed at the vulnerable instant when he checked his rush to swerve out toward the ballcarrier. The Orphan right end slammed a clean block against his legs. Clint went down hard. He was still on the ground when Ricker galloped past him on his way to pay dirt. Stan Flack booted the extra point. The score was 7-0.

CHAPTER 14

The early touchdown shocked the Rebels, a normal enough reaction, as Clint knew. He was immediately concerned, however, with how deep the shock had penetrated. Was it bad enough to shake their confidence? Bad enough to dull the edge of their determination?

Yancy solved the question with an angry comment. "We're stupid!" he burst out. "Just plain stupid! They played us for the morons that we are, and they'll do it again if we don't start using our brains instead of acting like a bunch of sheep."

"It was my fault," Clint said flatly. "I was the deep man. If I hadn't let myself get sucked in I might have stopped him."

It was a shrewd statement, shrewder than Clint had anticipated. It brought an immediate reaction.

"Nuts!" said Archer angrily. "We *all* handed 'em that touchdown. Like Yancy said, we're stupid. Me, I'm goin' to try to use my head for something beside line butting."

"Yeah," growled Hank Steuben, the big center. "If we're going to admit this early in the game that they're smarter than we are, we might as well walk in and take our showers."

Clint expelled a relieved breath. The Rebels' shock was wearing off faster than he had dared hope. A reliable antidote, anger at themselves, was moving in to take its place. Clint gave the men a parting booster shot. "We'll get that touchdown back," he said, with all the confidence he could put into the words.

Big talk. Too big? Clint was not entirely sure. He only knew he had to make himself believe, and the other Rebels, too, that they were far from licked. He also knew it could only be accomplished through a show of offensive power, which would supply the definite conviction that the Rebels could also move the ball. An immediate touchdown was not, of course, an absolute essential. The vital element, to be determined in the next few minutes, was to give the Rebels confidence in their attack.

It was Clint's responsibility. He was the man who

would have to call the shots. He fought off doubt as he waited for the kickoff. What sort of offensive did the Rebels really have? It had never been tested in actual competition. He thrust the thought aside as he wiped damp palms against his pants. He would not have to wait long for the answer.

The kick came off Flack's toe. The guy was an accomplished booter. The ball came high and deep, directly toward Clint Martin, waiting on the goal line. He swallowed the lump of panic in his throat, relaxed as well as he could, and made the catch. He let out a grateful grunt to find the ball safely in his hands. The ball cradled in his arm, he started upfield, no longer plagued by panic.

He studied the Rebels' blocking in the brief time permitted him, noting that though erratic, it was not as bad as he had feared it might be. The men to his right seemed to be having better luck, so he swerved in that direction, and found an opening which took him to the twenty-four-yard line before the Orphans pulled him down. It was not a spectacular runback, but Clint felt it was more than adequate. It could have been a whole lot worse.

It required little knowledge of psychology for Clint to figure out the impact that a successful opening play would have upon the Rebels. He had a strong conviction, too, that such a play should involve as many members of the team as possible, a running play rather than a pass play, in which Clint and Yancy would be the two key figures.

He made his decision swiftly, calling the play with no show of hesitation. The Rebels left the huddle and scooted for the line with the air of men hungry for raw meat. Clint stood for an instant behind his center, Hank Steuben, glancing to right and left to see that his ends were properly split. Then he reached down for the ball.

Steuben slapped it in his hands. Clint held it balanced in his fingers while he faded toward the side line, making a good show of trying to spot a receiver. He waited until the guard had cut across behind the line to join the blocking. Then Clint took stock of things in front of him. He liked what he saw.

It was a keeper all the way. The fake pass had loosened up the Orphan backfield, giving the men in front of Clint the chance to pick their targets. An Orphan lineman almost got through in time to nail Clint before he made his turn. Clint sidestepped the lunging tackle, regained balance, and began to move behind his blockers.

The Rebels did a fine job, taking advantage of the fact that Clint had made it easier for them by avoiding the experienced Flack, at the other end of the line. They mowed a path. They could not have accomplished it against more seasoned opposition, but they looked good just the same.

When the blocking wore thin, Clint was on his own. He made the most of it, aided by the stimulating knowledge that the Rebels' first ground play was a success. He swerved and cat-hopped through the Orphan backfield. Stan Flack came across to pull him down.

The run had chalked up fourteen yards for a first down. The Rebels came back into the huddle slightly dazed. Their expressions said, "Are we *that* good?" Clint gave them no time to reach the conclusion that they were better than they really were. The play, to be sure, had clicked, yet Clint knew full well that an element of luck is always present in plays requiring close precision. The men had had their luck and it had served its purpose. Clint had been lucky too. He had gambled and had won. No one could make the Rebels believe now that the Orphans had too great an edge on them, despite the presence of Britt and Flack.

Clint forced himself to remember that the Orphans, at this stage of the game, were facing the same problem the Rebels had faced earlier. They were thoroughly unfamiliar with what the Rebels had to offer in the way of an offensive strategy, and in a way their handicap was even greater. The Rebels had been warned of Britt and Flack. The Orphans had to learn the hard way about Rebels who might be considered dangerous.

Following the thought to its logical conclusion, Clint knew he had to take all possible advantage of a period that promised to be brief. The Rebels had gathered a lot of information during their defensive stint, so it was reasonable to assume the Orphans would learn too. The thing to do now was to keep them guessing and unbalanced while they learned.

Clint gathered, by their taut, nervous gestures, that the Orphans had been slightly shaken. They would be overeager now, he reasoned, determined to break up the next play before it could get started.

The Rebels had mastered, or had tried to master, one simple little draw play, and this, Clint hoped, was the time to try it out while the Orphans were still trying to control their nerves. He called the play, splitting his ends again as a diversion tactic.

The Rebels came fast from their huddle to the line of scrimmage. The Orphans across the line were quivering with eagerness. Clint took the snap from center, faded a few steps as if to pass, then shoveled a short pass to his fullback, Andy Beal.

Dukes, the left guard, after token resistance, permitted the opposing guard to come charging wild-eyed through the line. Nat Page, a good blocking back, timed his move just right. He came in low and hard to mouse-trap the charging Orphan guard out of the play, leaving a sizable hole in the line.

Clint whipped through the hole first, leading Beal, the ballcarrier, into the Orphan backfield. Clint knocked one defender out of position with a brush block, then hurled himself into the midsection of another Orphan. Andy Beal, though not in a class with Britt, could back his two-hundred pounds with a fair amount of speed. He used it now, bulling his way for seven yards before they pulled him down.

The Orphans called time out—a wise move to give themselves a chance to settle down and to recover from surprise. It seemed certain that they had not expected the Rebels to come up with such offensive strength. Clint, as a matter of fact, had not expected it either, and he warned himself not to be too optimistic. He also warned the other Rebels. An Orphan replacement came in bearing instructions from the bench. A replacement also came in for the Rebels.

"Shag wants you to keep your ends wide on every formation," he told Clint. "It will force Flack to move wide, too, and keep him out of our hair as much as possible. Shag also said not to try Flack's end on any wide plays. The guy's poison."

"What does he want me to run next?"

"He didn't say."

Clint nodded, believing he knew what Shag had in mind. He was leaving Clint on his own as long as possible, a move serving a dual purpose. It would give Shag a chance to learn how efficiently Clint could run a team. It would also help to boost Clint's confidence.

With the ball on the forty-five-yard stripe, second down, the Rebels needed three yards for a first down. Pass or run? It was a toss-up. Conservative reasoning called for a line play, and possibly another on the following down, under the assumption that any team worth its salt could grind out three yards for a first down in a couple of trys.

Clint shook off the temptation to be cautious. Though still a football novice, he knew enough about the game to recognize the value of surprise. The Orphans, he reasoned, would accept the possibility of a pass but probably would not be expecting one, having reason to believe that a team of the Rebels' caliber could not produce a passer of any real ability. So Clint called a signal for a pass.

When the play got under way he found he had guessed wrong. The Orphan coach had probably gambled, too, instructing the Orphans to expect an overhead attack. Clint, fading at right angles to his line, got some protection as he looked downfield for a receiver, but found no one who was not covered like a tent. Flack had things well under control in this area, and a backfield man was clinging to Yancy like a burr as Yancy sprinted down the side line.

It should have been a set up for a keeper play, except that the left side of the Rebel line had failed to hold the fort. A pair of Orphan linemen were converging on Clint, making it doubtful that he could get back to the line of scrimmage.

Shooting another desperate look downfield, Clint saw Yancy's arm come up in a commanding gesture toward the center of the field, his back still to Clint. Clint believed he knew what Yancy had in mind. There was no time for second guessing, so Clint took the chance, rifling a hard one toward a point ahead of Yancy and about ten yards inside the line.

It may have been telepathy or merely a great football instinct. Yancy, at any rate, swerved at the right instant, cutting sharply to his left, away from the man who had him covered. He turned his head in time to spot the ball, shot his big hands out, and grabbed it. The effort staggered him just long enough to let the defending Orphan bring him down on the Orphan twenty-four-yard line. The catch had been terrific and the pass had been terrific. It was big-league all the way.

Clint was still shaking his head with wonder as he started for the huddle. That play had been a honey, a long-shot gamble that clicked; he had never heaved a better pass. He tried to weigh the element of luck behind it. Assuming that a lot of it really was luck, he asked himself how long the luck would last.

The Rebels themselves were not fools enough to believe a thing like that could happen every time. The fact, though, that it had happened at all gave them the terrific boost of thinking that the odds were with them, a valuable asset to any team.

Whatever belief in their invincibility the Rebels might have held was soon wiped out. Clint called a line play which might easily have worked, because the hole was there. It was a cutback inside tackle. Clint scooped the ball to Archer, who got the pigskin in his mitts and fumbled it. Clint dove for the bobbling ball and curled himself around it as the Orphans piled on top of him. The ball was spotted for a two-yard loss.

"I muffed it!" Tom Archer said, with stricken eyes.

"Forget it!" Clint snapped. "And forget it fast! Fumbling is part of football."

"But at *this* time!" Archer moaned.

"If you think you're not good enough for us, I'll have Shag take you out," Clint told him harshly.

Sanity returned to Archer's eyes. "I'll stick around," he said sheepishly.

Clint gave him no time to brood over the fumble. He called Archer's signal in the huddle—for the same play that had just been bungled. From a tactical standpoint it was not the proper play, because it was not designed for long yardage, which the Rebels needed. Clint knew this, but he made the decision anyway, feeling that an immediate vote of confidence to Tom Archer was essential. It was another gamble.

It paid off. Archer gathered in Clint's accurate flip. He hit the small hole like a bullet, powered by a resolve to make up for his fumble on the previous down. He kept on scrambling for yardage, forcing Clint to believe that he had called a smart play, after all. The Orphans, obviously not expecting a repeat performance, were thrown off balance long enough for Archer to peel off nine yards.

On third down, three to go, Clint judged the temper of his fired-up linemen, believing they could carry him to a first down on a quarterback sneak—and they did. Hank Steuben charged like a wild bull, with Clint right on his heels. Faber and Dukes, on either side of Hank, kept tacklers from barging in. The gain was short but adequate. Clint had a foot to spare.

The Rebels had the ball, first down, on the Orphan fourteen-yard line. From here in, the going would be rough, because the Orphans could concentrate their defense in a limited area. They no longer had to watch for a long pass, and their backfield men could remain more mobile in defense of running plays.

Clint sent Andy Beal into the line, discovering that the Orphan forward wall was also dangerously fired up. The gain went for three yards—not enough. Clint tried to reach Yancy in the end zone with a pass. An Orphan defender knocked it down. Another line play ground out two more yards. Fourth down—five desperately long yards remaining for a first down.

Clint wanted instruction from the bench. Shag, however, sat tight, letting Clint sweat this one out alone. It would have to be a pass, of course—maybe a short one across the line, just long enough for the first down. He was weighing the chances when an upsetting thought occurred to him, making him wonder why his brain had been working in such a shallow groove. If he was thinking automatically in terms of a pass, it was only common sense to assume that the Orphans were thinking the same way.

He called the signal in the huddle, trying to keep his voice as steady and full of confidence as possible. He called his own signal for an end run following a fake pass.

"Break through," he told his linemen. "I don't think they'll tumble to it soon enough."

They nodded, knowing what he meant. A lineman, by entering the opposing backfield on a pass play could draw a penalty for his team. An alert defense, seeing a lineman come through, would know instantly that it had to be a running play. Clint was gambling on his belief that the Orphans lacked the experience and seasoning to analyze the play in time to change their tactics.

The play got off to a smooth start. Fading fast toward the side line, Clint put on a good show of looking frantically for a receiver. The Orphans spread out just as frantically, to cover every eligible man in sight.

When Clint cut in, a couple of sharp blocks from his own backfield men gave him some running room. He crossed the scrimmage line wide open. Enough of the Rebel linemen had broken through to do a lot of damage in the Orphan backfield, while Clint, running with restrained speed, tried to take advantage of every opening as he wheeled and twisted on his way to pay dirt.

An Orphan hit him from the side before he reached the goal line. The tackle, though, was panicky and high. The Orphan landed on Clint's back, clinging like a monkey. Clint staggered under the impact, yet managed to keep his feet. He made a final, violent lunge before he hit the ground. The ball was on the goal line, and that was all that mattered.

The Rebels acted like a pack of maniacs. The Orphans were concerned and thoughtful, taking time to revise their opinion of the Rebels. Yancy held on the try for extra point, and Clint booted a clean one through the uprights to tie the score at 7-7.

CHAPTER
15

When the Rebels started upfield for the kickoff, Clint, for the first time, became aware of the crowd. It would have been difficult to ignore it now, because the fans had given up their attitude of watchful waiting. There was a quality of disbelief in their yells, also a growing excitement as they permitted themselves to hope that the Rebels might have a fighting chance against the Orphans.

The fans saw a lot of football during the remainder of the half. It could not, by any stretch of imagination, have been labeled expert football, but this failed to dampen the enthusiasm of the fans. They were watching a pair of courageous, fighting teams, a privilege which offset imperfections such as fumbles, penalties, and frequent clumsy teamwork.

The Rebels battled gamely, fighting for each yard they gained and contesting each yard they surrendered. The game began to fall into a pattern—one which Clint faced with grim reluctance. He did not try to kid himself with senseless optimism. The Orphans had the better team.

The difference in the squads, Clint was sure, could be measured by the added strength that Britt and Flack imparted to the Orphans. Aside from the two varsity men Clint believed the Rebels had an edge in coaching and material. There was little consolation in the belief.

The Orphans scored another touchdown in the second period. They tried a two-point conversion, but failed to pull it off. They lost an almost certain additional touchdown by a critical fifteen-yard penalty that was called against them. The score was 13-7 at the end of the half.

The Rebels, too obviously, were fighting against discouragement as they plodded to the dressing room. Shag Conway lightened their gloom considerably, not by fight talk, but by his own unworried air.

"They're a little better than I figured them to be," he said. "However, if they didn't have Britt and Flack we could lick 'em, not that it's any encouragement to you guys at the moment." Leaning, relaxed, against the wall, he went on. "You men have been playing good football, and I want you to keep it up. The Orphans haven't made any bad mistakes yet, but they're bound to. It's in the books, because they're as inexperienced as you are. When they do slip up it's a pretty safe bet that I'll be able to spot it. Just keep your teeth in that and hang on."

He turned to Yancy. "They've got a short lateral pass play to your side of the line that seems to have a hole in it. Ricker fakes a long pass, but his protection stays in place too long in order to make the fake look good. They get over too late to run good interference for the guy who takes the lateral. Keep that in mind, Yancy, and you may break through fast enough to pull one out of the hat."

When the game got under way again Clint became aware of a subtle change in the Orphans. Their play seemed smoother, more assured, as if they were convinced that they had finally hit their stride. This assurance should have worked against the Rebels, but it actually appeared to be operating in their favor. The Orphans, playing like men who were certain they could get another touchdown any time they needed it, had lost some of their early fire. They were bordering on overconfidence.

Their confidence appeared justified, particularly when they were on defense. They had gone far toward solving the Rebel attack. They had spotted Clint and Yancy as the two most dangerous men, and had modified their defense to keep the pair well covered. The third period remained scoreless.

Time was running out for the Rebels, who were becoming too well aware of this for their own good. They understood the disastrous consequences of defeat, and under the resulting pressure their play began to suffer.

The tension was unexpectedly relieved, however, early in the final period. The Orphans had run a punt back to their thirty-one-yard line where, full of confidence, they settled down on the offensive. The first play developed into a short lateral following a fake pass down the field. The formation was an exact blueprint of the one outlined by Shag, and Yancy had it spotted. He broke fast across the scrimmage line, and the protection around the passer arrived too late to take him out. Ricker's reactions were too slow. He did not see the peril until the ball had left his hand, and Yancy, travelling at full speed, picked the ball out of the air and kept on going.

The Orphans hadn't the slightest chance of reaching him. They gave chase after weathering their first violent shock, but Yancy crossed the goal line with yards of daylight behind him. The Orphans, stunned by the suddenness of the catastrophe, received another shock when Clint kicked the extra point, putting the Rebels in the lead, 14-13.

The touchdown pumped new life into the Rebels. Their tension, though undiminished, assumed a different form. Their play was better coordinated now, as the crippling handicap of desperation was removed. They were back in the game again, with an actual chance to win, which made a big difference. They went down under the kickoff like men fresh from a long rest.

The shoe was on the other foot now. The pressure had been transferred from the Rebels to the Orphans, and Clint noted with regret that the Orphans stood the pressure well, obviously free, unlike the Rebels in a similar spot, from the numbing fear of losing. Some of their old fire returned. Two passes clicked in quick succession for a gain of nineteen yards.

Randy Keef came sprinting in to replace Dukes. Keef was excited, though he tried not to show it. Clint called time out, giving Keef ample time to deliver his message—a very important one.

"Shag has spotted something. Ricker has just started a nervous habit of wetting his fingers before he makes a pass."

"Just started it?" repeated Clint, puzzled. "Why hasn't he been doing it all along? It doesn't make much sense." After a thoughtful pause, however, he said,

"But maybe it does. Maybe it was an old habit they thought he was cured of. This is the first time he's been under any real pressure, so he could have gone back to it unconsciously. I hope his own coach doesn't notice it too soon."

Clint passed the priceless information on to the other men. The results of knowing exactly when a pass was on its way became evident at once, as the Orphans' overhead game struck a snag. The Orphan coach, probably intent on spotting weaknesses in the Rebel defense, failed to correct his quarterback's tip-off.

The game became a savage deadlock. The Orphans were battling for a win, but the Rebels were battling for their future, an added incentive which gave them the strength to keep the Orphans out of scoring territory.

Time was dragging for the Rebels and going much too fast to suit the Orphans. In the closing minutes of the game it began to look as if the Rebels had it made, but they suffered a disastrous setback while Clint was clinging to this desperate hope. The Rebels, in possession of the ball, were trying hard to freeze it, when a fumble in the line was recovered by the Orphans twenty-six yards from the Rebel goal line. The Orphans called time out. There were two minutes and fifteen seconds left to play. With luck, the Orphans could reach pay dirt in that time.

When play resumed the Rebels dug in grimly for a final stand. As the Orphans hurried from the huddle, Clint watched Ricker and saw that he was no longer wetting his fingers. It made sense to Clint. A few line plays might advance the ball far enough for the Orphans to attempt a winning field goal. Stan Flack was an excellent kicker.

It was not a running play. The Rebels were caught flat-footed when Ricker faded for a pass. Clint, with a gasp of horror, saw how badly he had been fooled. Flack was already streaking for the end zone, with no one to cover him. Clint was the only Rebel with a chance to get there—one chance in a thousand. He ran toward the danger spot, scarcely knowing he had started. Had the Rebels been tricked deliberately? It was quite possible. The finger wetting may have been done deliberately, to lay the groundwork for a situation just like this.

It was unimportant now, however, so Clint wiped all speculation from his mind to concentrate upon the job at hand. He was moving fast, covering ground with all the strength left in him. He kept his eye on Flack, a chance he had to take. He dared not break his stride by looking at the ball.

He saw Flack stop and wait, and noted the quick expression of concern on his face. Flack had arrived in time at the proper spot. The pass, though obviously accurate, was a fraction of a moment late, which gave Clint one last fighting chance.

He timed his backward glance just right. The ball was rifling toward Flack's upstretched hands. Clint leaped into the air, twisting as he went up, using his final ounce of energy. He felt the impact of the ball against his fingers and hung on, never knowing how he managed it. He felt a weight upon his back as Flack landed on him after a fruitless leap. The two men hit the ground together, but Clint had the ball locked firmly in his arms.

There were no more fumbles, no more problems during the few remaining moments of the game. When the Rebels took possession on the twenty-yard line, they successfully put the pigskin in a deep freeze until the final whistle blew.

There was no hilarity or wild celebration in the Rebel dressing room. None of the Rebels seemed inclined toward noise or horseplay. Their emotions went too deep for that. By united effort, they had accomplished the impossible. They did not have to tell one another what had happened. They all knew. The exchange of slow, contented grins was ample for the moment, yet the strange silence of the dressing room was charged to the bursting point with happiness and pride. The feeling of festivity would soon take over, but not until each man had enjoyed this moment to its fullest.

When Clint and Yancy left the field, they walked for some distance without speaking.

"That was a squeaker," Yancy said at last, and his voice was unsteady. "I'm getting a delayed reaction. I didn't have time to be scared while we were playing, but I'm scared now."

"I'm sort of weak myself," admitted Clint.

"Do you think Crawford would have lowered the boom in spite of the good showing we made?"

"Yes," said Clint. "I think he would have done just that. It was a matter of principle with him."

"Well, we cleared the first big hurdle, anyway. The next one may not be so high."

"Just keep your fingers crossed," said Clint.

The people who had seen the Rebel-Orphan game were quick to pass the word that something fresh and different had appeared upon Midwestern's campus—a revitalized Rebel team worth watching. Their next practice session drew a larger crowd of fans than had ever shown up before.

It was no surprise to anyone when more of the Rebel deserters made a hang-dog appearance, asking for reinstatement in the fold, willing to admit their decision had been hasty. They were gladly received, particularly those who were willing to supply their own outfits.

The Rebels were inclined to preen themselves a bit over their recent victory, but Shag gave them no time for strutting. He stepped up the tempo of the workouts, driving the men hard, because he knew they were willing to be driven now.

CHAPTER
16

Shoo-fly Finnigan retained his status as one of the
Rebels' most loyal fans. He no longer sat aloof upon his
scooter; he parked it now and walked up and down the
side line, following the play.

Clint took the risk one day of violating Shoo-fly's
privacy. He approached the old man, saying casually,
"The boys seem to be shaping up."

Bracing himself for a caustic answer, Clint was
caught off base when Shoo-fly faced him, tilted his
derby toward the back of his head, and said mildly,
"Sure looks like it. The linemen are beginning to use
the right sort of leverage."

Clint's jaw sagged before he could control it.

Shoo-fly scowled. "Don't you think I know leverage when I see it?" he demanded. "I've worked with

men all my life. There's even a proper way to lift a shovelful of dirt."

"Yeah, sure there is," Clint hastily agreed.

Shoo-fly glared another moment before saying gruffly, "All right, all right, don't be so smug. When I make a mistake I'm willing to admit it. I hated football because I didn't understand it, so I read books about it, studied the rules, and watched you boys at work. Good game."

Before Clint could form a suitable comment with regard to Shoo-fly's great discovery, Shoo-fly changed the subject. He nodded toward a small group standing apart from the other fans. "Have you been giving any thought to those lads?" he inquired.

Glancing in the direction of Shoo-fly's nod, Clint saw a watchful group standing apart from the others. Though shrunken from its previous size, it was composed of the die-hard hecklers who apparently refused to believe the Rebels were no longer vulnerable.

"Yes," said Clint, "I have. They're here almost every day. They just stand around and don't make any noise. They remind me of buzzards in a dead tree."

"That's what I mean," said Shoo-fly. "I think they're hatching something, and I don't mean eggs."

Clint had reached the same conclusion, for he was reasonably certain that these men would not give up easily. The blanks they had drawn in previous at-

tempts against Clint and the Rebels were sure to stimu-
late their vindictiveness. It was something for Clint to
keep in mind, but this proved difficult under the
mounting pressure of the Rebels' preparation for their
next game against a team which called itself the Rag-
tags.

After their last workout Shag said, "I've got only
one worry. I'm afraid you fellows are a little too cocky.
Confidence is fine if you don't let it run away with you.
The Rag-tags, from everything we can learn about
them, don't have much of a team. Certainly they're not
in a class with the Orphans. However, just remember
that you didn't have much of a team either, so don't sell
the Rag-tags short. They might be tough, and you'll all
be smart if you figure it that way. Don't forget that
anything can happen in a football game."

There was no way for Clint to know how strongly
the other Rebels had been affected by Shag's advice. He
only knew that the advice had not been wasted upon
him. Once again his responsibility as quarterback bore
down on him. The Rag-tags might be pushovers. On
the other hand, they might not be. In the latter case it
would be up to Clint to pull the strings that would keep
the Rebels in existence—at least for the remainder of
the season.

He tried to study on the night before the game,
promptly encountering the same turbulence of thought

which had bogged him down the week before. Then, recalling the restful influence of the deserted stadium, he started once more in that direction, hoping the effect would be the same tonight.

His hope was brief. The field was dimly lighted by a quarter moon, but the light which swiftly caught Clint's eye did not come from the moon. It came in intermittent flashes from the far end of the field, where there was a small building used to house dressing rooms.

Clint's immediate reaction, a flood of anger, set his feet in motion, sending him on a dead run toward the spot. The sprint lasted long enough to shake his thoughts in place and to impart a sense of caution to his first wild dash which could have easily taken him into something he was not equipped to handle. Good sense warned him to find out what was going on before he charged like a goaded bull into a mess of trouble.

He changed course, moving swiftly, but with more caution, toward the deep shadow of the bleachers on the east side of the field. Following the shadow, he came closer to the building, when his anger once more threatened to overcome his common sense.

A small pickup truck was parked outside the door. Five or six dim figures were making hurried trips inside the building and back to the truck, using flashlights as sparingly as possible. They had obviously broken the padlock from the door, and the reason for this was not hard to guess. They were stealing the Rebel's uniforms, tossing them frantically into the body of the truck.

For the fraction of an instant Clint almost lost his self-control. He was crouched and ready for a one-man charge when his good sense won the battle by a scanty margin. It is doubtful that the thieves, at this stage, could have been scared off by a single man. Certainly they could not have been overpowered. Having gone this far, their vindictiveness, or whatever compelled them, would surely force them to complete the job. Clint figured it that way, at any rate.

He also knew he was completely helpless at this distance from the building. Getting closer might provide him with some sort of break, though he could not imagine what the break could be. The odds were against him, as, still hugging the shadows, he reached the near end of the building, his mind devoid of any plan of action.

The thieves, though nervous, seemed to be enjoying themselves. Clint heard the subdued laughs of men who thought they were doing something very clever and could hardly wait for the results. He risked a peek around the corner of the building, feeling no surprise at all when he recognized several of the chronic troublemakers who had been in the Rebels' hair since the start of the season.

Loading the uniforms was a short job. The time of Clint's arrival could hardly have been more exact—a source of scant satisfaction to him now. Whipping his brain into high gear had small effect. Nothing occurred to him but hopeless hare-brained schemes. As a last resort he would of course, come out of hiding and start fighting even though the effort could accomplish little more than providing an outlet for his rage. It could also serve to get him badly mauled, a belated thought which came in time to make him hesitate just long enough to get the break he needed.

When the uniforms were loaded in the truck a canvas covering was tossed across them. Two men climbed into the cab, and while Clint was wondering what would happen to the others, they started jogging from the field as if following a previously rehearsed plan.

Clint reasoned hopefully that he could handle two men more easily than half a dozen. He was gathering himself for the attack when his mind grabbed suddenly at an obvious fact he should have noticed earlier. The position of the truck was such that it would have to back in a half turn before starting from the field, and the turn would move the end of the truck toward Clint.

When the driver backed the truck Clint did not hesitate. A new plan flashed into his mind like the inspiration of a genius. The other men were still within calling distance of the men in the cab in the event of an attack by Clint. What, then, could be more practical than to join the expedition? If his luck still held he would be taken to the spot where the uniforms would either be hidden or destroyed, and there would still be only two men to contend with.

Clint made his move as quickly and as smoothly as he could. He had an uneasy moment when his added weight, as he climbed across the tailboard, made the springs joggle. He breathed more easily when the driver started forward, probably believing that the wheels had stuck a rough spot on the ground. It was a simple matter for Clint to fashion a deep nest in the uniforms, then pull the canvas back across him.

The truck was still upon the field when Clint began to realize that a nest of football uniforms, though comfortable, presents a drawback. The uniforms had all been cleaned last week, but that was six days ago. Clint hastily squirmed to the edge of the canvas covering, made a small opening for his head, and found the fresh air extremely welcome.

What sort of reasoning, he wondered, would make these guys pull a stunt like this? Pure vindictiveness undoubtedly had a part in it—the urge to swing a low punch at the Rebels, who had clobbered them on one occasion and made fools of them on another.

Perhaps they had been willing to gamble that this raid on the uniforms would put permanent skids under the Rebels. They could logically assume that the Athletic Department would refuse to furnish the Rebels with uniforms for the Rag-tag game, and that the businesses, even if they were so inclined, could not replace the outfits for some time. There was also the possibility that Herbert Crawford would use the incident as a technical loophole to crack down on the Rebels, basing his decision on the fact that they had not won their next scheduled game, according to Crawford's stipulation. Whatever the outcome, it was certain that this stunt, if successful, would deal the Rebels a crippling blow.

But there was no certainty at this point that it would be successful. Clint was well satisfied as he considered his position in the drama. The advantage of surprise would be entirely his, and the odds were not formidable at all. The two men in the truck's cab were not very big. Clint had taken careful note of this. They were not football men, tough and seasoned by past weeks of scrimmage. It ought to be a breeze.

But after riding so high his assurance began to hit a down grade. It happened gradually, but it became very low indeed when he finally was convinced that the truck was being followed by a car. It accepted the truck's sedate pace and made each turn behind the truck before it reached the open highway.

Clint realized now that he had been an optimistic chump. The rest of the raiders, of course, were in the car, trailing their pilfered cargo to its destination. The car had obviously been parked outside the field.

Clint's situation had changed abruptly. It was now a mess. The odds had reverted to their original quotation, six to one. Clint found himself perspiring freely despite the coolness of the night.

Grimly figuring his chances, he found them very slim. He finally decided he could pin his hopes on just one thing. It depended entirely on what happened at the end of the line. If both the truck and the car stopped in the right positions he might be able, by moving fast, to slide from his nest and reach the ground without being seen. If he could remain unseen he would then possess a lot of valuable knowledge. He would know where the uniforms were hidden.

By keeping a mound of the canvas cover in front of his face he was able to prevent the men behind from spotting him in the headlights of the car. He was also able to get a good idea of the route the truck was taking. That, too, would be helpful, in the improbable event that he could get back to town with the information.

The possibility that he might accomplish this was

getting slimmer by the minute. His hopes were dragging bottom, when they suddenly took an upward zoom. The car turned off. It was several moments before Clint realized that the headlights were no longer following the truck. The men behind had obviously been acting merely as a convoy to assure the safety of the truck while it was passing through the town. Once on the outskirts, it was assumed that the driver and his helper would have passed the danger zone and that the disposal of the uniforms, from that point on, would be a two-man job.

Clint's nervous tension eased considerably. The odds, though still against him, were a lot more favorable. He began to lay some optimistic plans, and then realized that he was wasting time. It would be wiser, he reflected, to wait until the showdown time arrived. He might have to call a change in signals if the opposing team suddenly shifted its defense. He decided, therefore, to let circumstances govern his choice of plays.

The trip was shorter than he had expected. He judged the distance roughly as a mile or so beyond the outskirts of the town. The truck slowed down and doused its headlights before turning into a bumpy dirt road, obviously a neglected farm lane.

It was safe now for Clint to lift his head into the open. He studied his surroundings, reasonably certain of the location. It was a small, unworked farm south of town. The house, he had been told, had burned down several years ago. The discouraged owners had moved away. The property had remained unsold, and the rickety old barn would be an ideal place to hide the uniforms.

Clint's immediate problems came to a quick head as the truck pulled up before the barn and stopped. When the motor was turned off, the silence was alarming. Clint fought the urge to hold his breath. The two men in the front seat appeared to be affected that way too. For several seconds there was no sound or motion from that area. Then they both hurried into action.

A voice, strained and nervous, said, "Let's dump these blasted uniforms. This place gives me the creeps."

Clint had sense enough to remain quiet until he felt a movement in the truck. When the springs began to stir a bit he tried to make his own moves as smooth and unnoticeable as possible. He came to a crouch, and because it seemed like a good idea at the moment, he grabbed an armful of the uniforms. When the first man came alongside the body of the truck, Clint let out a yell, making it as bloodcurdling as he could. At the same time he tossed the uniforms over the head of the nearest man.

The element of surprise and the paralyzing yell were more effective than Clint could have hoped. The first man fought against the uniforms as if they were a pile of snakes. The other man stood frozen in his tracks, remaining in that position while Clint vaulted from the truck and landed right in front of him. The fellow's eyes bugged out as if Clint were a man from outer space.

Clint, knowing that he was acting like a sentimental fool, could not bring himself to throw a punch while the poor guy was helpless, like a sitting duck. He waited an instant, therefore, until the other man, moved by the instinct of self-preservation, threw a wild punch of his own. Clint ducked the swing and, with a clear conscience, nailed the uniform snatcher with a wallop to the jaw which sent him down and out.

Clint, whirling to deal with the other man, found he had delayed too long, a delay which threatened to be costly. The man had freed himself of the uniforms and, lacking the desire to be a hero of the fighting type, had chosen a more practical solution of his problem. He was scrambling behind the wheel of the truck by the time Clint reached him.

Clint tried to pull him out, but the man clung grimly to the wheel. When it was evident that he had no chance to start the truck and make a getaway, he used his head and pulled a cagey stunt. Snatching the key from the ignition lock, he hurled it far into the deep weeds near the truck.

Clint made an involuntary move toward the spot, before realizing that he would have had a better chance to find a needle in a haystack. He considered the situation briefly before resorting to logic. "O.K., mister," he conceded. "I can't get the uniforms away from here in the truck and neither can you. However, I've got the rest of the night to pry you out of that seat and beat the daylights out of you. You've got a choice. You can come down peaceably and let me tie you up or you can take what you deserve. You've got ten seconds to think it over."

The uniform snatcher cut the time limit by five seconds. He came down meekly and submitted meekly to the trussing. Clint went about the job efficiently, using the flexible nylon belts from the football pants. The other man presented no problem either. Still groggy from Clint's fist he was soon securely bound. Clint, in a charitable moment, hoisted them both into the truck, where they would be reasonably comfortable on the uniforms.

Clint glanced at his watch before starting back toward town. He looked again, more closely, finding it hard to believe that so little time had passed. It seemed hours since he had left his room, yet the hour was still comparatively early—a quarter to eleven.

He walked fast, curbing an impatience which

made him want to run. He had to remind himself that he had a game to play tomorrow, a game which now would surely be played. He forced his mind to the more practical problem of the moment. He would have to find a way to get the uniforms back where they belonged.

He had reached the town and was walking on the sidewalk when he heard a small commotion just ahead. The remarks, coming from a single person, were picturesque and sincere. It was not hard to recognize the voice, and Clint did so with a feeling of quick satisfaction, knowing that his problem was as good as solved.

Shoo-fly, it appeared, had run out of gas and was telling his scooter what he thought of it. "Blasted contraption!" he shouted. "If I could feed you hay, a thing like this would never happen!"

Clint asked, "Can I help?"

Shoo-fly whirled. "Who're you?" he demanded. Then, recognizing Clint, he said, "You ought to be in bed. You've got a game tomorrow. What're you doing here at this time of night?"

Clint told him briefly, while Shoo-fly made rumbling noises in his throat. When Clint had finished, Shoo-fly said, "O.K., son, I'll take over. You go to bed. I'll get the police."

"I'd rather not bring in the police, sir," Clint said promptly.

"Why not?"

"It might be a mistake to make such a big issue of it. The Rebels are still skating on thin ice, and I don't think it would be smart to advertise the fact that we managed to get ourselves into more trouble. The news will leak out, of course, but it might be worse for us if it became a matter for the law to settle."

Shoo-fly thought it over before nodding. "Well, you're shaving it pretty thin, but I guess you've got a point."

They walked the short distance into town, where Shoo-fly found a drugstore telephone and put the wheels in motion. He tried to chase Clint home to bed, then grudgingly accepted Clint's refusal.

Another pickup truck, driven by one of Shoo-fly's husky young employees, was soon on the scene. They returned to the barn, where, after a few select words from Shoo-fly, the prisoners were released for their walk back to town. The uniforms were loaded and returned to the dressing room.

"You'll spend the night here," Shoo-fly told the young man who had brought the truck. "I don't think they'll try again, but there's no sense taking chances. I'll send a few more of the boys out here to keep you company."

Then he turned to Clint. *"Now* will you go home and get some sleep?"

"Yes, sir. And thanks."

"For what?" demanded Shoo-fly crustily. "Go home! Scat!"

CHAPTER
17

The Rebels did not learn until the following day that calamity had missed them by a narrow margin, and the news, as it turned out, was beneficial. Their outrage was still undiluted when they went into the game. They expended their anger on the hapless Rag-tags, who had scant time to wonder what the Rebels were so sore about. The final score was 25-7.

Clint was granted only a brief time to enjoy the security which the Rag-tag game assured the Rebels. The security might be only temporary with no promise that it would last beyond the present season. He had hoped to be able to enjoy this period, to close his mind to the probable future of the Rebels, and to get the most out of the present—a hope which was denied him by a complication he had not foreseen. It threw him into a tail spin of anger and resentment.

The news was broken to him at another conference in Grant's office. Clint obeyed the summons with the usual apprehension such conferences built in him, knowing that the meeting had to do with the welfare of the Rebels. Maggie Parnell's presence confirmed this.

Grant began by saying, "Looks like you boys are about to have another playmate."

Grant's tone put Clint on guard. "Who?" he inquired warily.

Grant took a deep breath, looked at the ceiling, and said, "Bronco Slade."

Clint jerked forward in his chair. "You're kidding!" he accused.

"No," said Maggie. "He's not kidding."

Clint left his chair as if the seat had become red-hot. "That slob!" he exploded. "I wouldn't let him mess up the Rebels if we all had to play on crutches!"

"Simmer down," said Maggie patiently. "Roger and I both know how you feel and we agree with you. This, however, is a matter of policy. Cool off, Clint, and listen to the rest of it."

Clint resumed his chair, mildly ashamed of his outburst. "Shoot," he said.

"It's like this," continued Maggie. "Bronco's no

bargain as a person, and his swelled head is making him worse all the time. However, he is a football player, a good one, our best quarterback. At the moment he's flunking a course in economics and has become ineligible for football. That's one of the few things the Athletic Department can't lick."

"What's that got to do with the Rebels?"

"Plenty. The Dean has agreed to reinstate Bronco's eligibility in a couple of weeks if he can bone up and pass an exam. We're assigning a tutor to him, and he's worried enough now so that we're sure he'll buckle down and study. Meanwhile we want him to keep in shape. He's barred from our line-up, so that leaves the Rebels, over whom we are supposed to have no jurisdiction. Bronco has had orders to volunteer."

Clint devoted a few moments to annoyed thought. "Do we have to accept him?" he asked finally.

"No," said Maggie promptly. "However, I'd like to point out again that it's a matter of policy. I don't have to tell you that conditions are . . . well, let's call them strained . . . between the Athletic Department and the Rebels. We are, in effect, asking a favor of you, and it might ease the situation a little if you went along with the big brass. Do you agree, Roger?"

"I think it would be smart," said Grant.

After another brief silence Clint gave in. "You're

both right, of course. We'll work it out. Tell the fathead to report this afternoon."

So Bronco joined the Rebels. He wore his varsity uniform, determined to be set apart as much as possible from the rabble he had been forced to join. He assumed an air of amused superiority—the air of an adult playing with a lot of little boys. Clint had had time to warn the Rebels in advance, gaining their reluctant promise of cooperation.

Clint tried to start the experiment as peacefully as possible. "We're glad to have you with us, Bronco," he forced himself to say.

"I'll *bet* you are," said Bronco nastily, ignoring the olive branch. "From what I've heard, you guys could use a football player."

Clint struggled with his good intentions but lost the unequal fight. His eyes chilled off. "Is that the way you want it?" he asked evenly.

Bronco took his time before replying. He looked Clint over carefully, noting the even distribution of the added weight. It made a difference, and the difference showed beneath the studied insolence of Bronco Slade's expression. He said at last, "Yeah, that's the way I want it."

So that was the way he got it. The Rebels ignored

him in a manner which was not assumed, a condition Bronco made no attempt to remedy. He seemed contented in the belief that he was the best man on the field, an accepted fact which he did not have to prove.

This became evident in scrimmage. He condescended to play fullback, accepting the fact that he could not be effective in his usual quarterback spot until he became more familiar with the Rebels' signals. His play was lackadaisical, interrupted by occasional attempts at clowning, obviously intended to create the impression that he could not be expected to exert much effort in such a silly cause.

There was one exception to his careless play. At a time when he was carrying the ball he found a wide hole in the opposing backfield. Seeing that the hole would lead him through to Clint, he opened the throttle, giving it everything he had—which was considerable.

He made no attempt to swerve, a challenge Clint accepted, as he took a few swift steps to gain momentum. When he threw his tackle it was accurate and hard. Clint knew, this time, what he was doing. This was different from the previous time, when Bronco had tried to trample him into the turf. Experience and twenty extra pounds had made a change.

Bronco learned it the hard way. He hit the ground like a lassoed calf. Gulping for air, he glared at Clint. Clint was also shaken up, but he tried hard not to show it. He jumped to his feet, shot an indifferent glance at Bronco, turned on his heel, and walked away.

Clint made an accurate guess that Bronco would not try again. It was one thing to be downed in that manner by an all-American, another thing entirely to be slapped down by a nobody. It was a tarnish to his reputation that Bronco dared not face again, so he tried to cover his chagrin with even broader clowning, a performance that did not appeal to Shag or to the Rebels.

Shag stopped the play. "You've put your act across," he said to Bronco. "We all get the idea now— you're too good to play on this squad. It happens, though, that we take our football seriously, even if it's just kid stuff to you." Shag made his statement quietly and turned away.

Bronco's quick temper flared, showed in his eyes an instant, then turned to sullenness. Clint watched with grim amusement, understanding Bronco Slade's frustration. Bronco knew he would be a fool to tangle with Shag Conway, who outranked him in reputation and who could outplay him in every department of the game. It was a spot in which Bronco was forced to swallow his anger and resentment. His performance for the remainder of the day was deliberately lethargic without, however, any more attempt at clowning.

After the workout Shag called Clint aside. "I went

easy on the guy today," said Shag. "I know we've got a ticklish situation on our hands, but just how much of his stuff are we supposed to take? I'll have to leave it up to you, Clint, because you've got more at stake than I have."

Clint thought for a moment. Then he said soberly, "I don't see how we can let him get by with it. If we do, it's bound to take some of the edge off the other men, and they're the ones we've got to think about. So far as I'm concerned, Shag, you can bear down on the jerk, treat him the way you'd treat any other goldbrick."

"That's all I need to know," said Shag with satisfaction.

Shag put the heat on Bronco during the few days preceding the next scheduled game. Bronco, far from happy, accepted the situation with what grace he could, held in line by his respect and awe of Shag. He played hard football, a performance that he seemed to feel had earned him extra consideration when the line-ups were posted for the game.

His hair-trigger temper got the better of him when he read the list. He whirled on Shag. "You mean I'm not playing quarterback today? I ought to be running this team and you know it!"

"If I knew it," Shag said quietly, "you'd be in there running it. You've had more general experience, I'll admit, but Clint has had more experience with this squad, and I'm sure he can get more out of the men than you can. You can help us a lot in the halfback spot."

Bronco thought it over angrily, trying, Clint decided, to come up with some fast angle that would justify him in refusing a subordinate spot in the Rebel backfield. While Bronco was still in this mood, Clint brought up another subject with explosive possibilities. "You'll also have to wear one of the Rebel uniforms," he said to Bronco.

"You're nuts!"

"It's part of our deal with the businesses who supplied us with the uniforms."

"Look, buster," said Bronco nastily, "you chumps can make clowns of yourselves if you want to, but you'll never get one of those dizzy shirts on *my* back!"

Clint let the ultimatum hang for several seconds, before asking quietly, "Is that final?"

"You bet it's final!" Bronco rasped.

"In which case," Clint said promptly, "you're all through. Get out and don't come back."

Bronco stared incredulously at Clint. His jaw sagged. Then astonishment gave way gradually to outrage. Clint watched it grow in Bronco's eyes. It was one thing to be seeking an excuse to quit the Rebels, another thing entirely to be booted from the team like an ordinary duffer, particularly when Clint happened to be the one to swing the boot.

Bronco moved a step toward Clint, his shoulders hunched, rage dancing in his eyes. It was a touchy moment, with violence in the air. Clint forced himself to stay relaxed and watchful, knowing that he could meet the challenge better that way.

The instant of greatest danger passed, betrayed by a subtle change in Bronco's eyes, as if a dormant thought had awakened. Clint guessed the nature of the thought—the disturbing memory of a wallop landed upon Bronco's jaw, a wallop uncorked by a man twenty pounds lighter than the man who faced Bronco now. Bronco was probably wondering how the added weight might affect another wallop. He did not permit himself to wonder very long.

"Thanks, buster," he said, managing to produce a harsh laugh. "You just did me a favor. The boys upstairs wouldn't like it much if I had climbed out of this menagerie by myself. It's different being tossed out. You let me off the hook, so thanks again."

"Don't mention it."

Bronco made his exit as dignified as possible. Clint watched him go, unable to dispute the truth of Bronco's parting words. The Rebels were delighted at the way things had turned out, and Clint felt this was not the time to disillusion them. They were primed for battle, which they demonstrated when they reached the field. They won a tough one, 18-12.

CHAPTER
18

Clint tried to minimize the probable effect of Bronco's brief association with the Rebels. It was not easy to shrug off. No matter how he tried to drape the incident with optimism, it all boiled down to the fact that Crawford had asked a favor of the Rebels, who, in effect, had told him to go jump in the lake. It was another black mark against the Rebels. How many black marks could they chalk up, Clint wondered dismally, and still hope to survive? Clint had to find out soon. The suspense was making him a nervous wreck. He called on Roger Grant.

Grant eyed him balefully and said, "You almost did it that time."

"Did he take it pretty hard?" asked Clint, gathering hope from the word *almost*.

"How did you expect him to take it?" Grant demanded irritably. "He's still sticking to his part of the bargain, but it was mighty close. What made you do a crazy thing like that?"

Clint sketched the details briefly. Grant shrugged. "I'd probably have done the same thing you did," he admitted. "That doesn't change the fact, however, that the Rebels' stock has taken another nose dive with the Athletic Department. Let's keep our fingers crossed."

"It may take more than that," Clint answered apprehensively.

Immediate developments did not ease Clint's apprehension. It was an ironic situation. The Rebels, looking better every day, began to roll, yet Clint's satisfaction in their progress was considerably dulled by long-range worry.

Max Hacker put Clint's worry into words, as Hacker doggedly maintained his feud with Grady Bell. "How much," demanded Hacker in his column, "can the Vulcans take? It is no laughing matter when a nationally known team plays second fiddle on its campus to a pick-up bunch of football players cavorting about in outlandish jerseys.

"Yet, my friends, that's exactly what is taking place. Call it a fad if you wish, but the Rebels, in some fantastic way, have captured the fancy of the student body and the local fans. We hear a lot of football talk.

And what do we hear most? Do we hear excited speculation as to how the Vulcans will make out in their next game? We hear a little to be sure, but what we hear is almost smothered by the more excited speculation as to how the Rebels will make out.

"Admittedly, the Vulcans, due to injuries and other unforeseen factors, are having a poor year. Can this explain, however, why the fans prefer to get steamed up over mediocre football instead of the top-notch brand? It's a mystery to us. Yet, mystery or not, one fact remains. The Rebels are stealing the football show. How much longer can the Vulcans take it?"

Clint read the article, slammed the paper on the floor, and kicked it. "The old so-and-so!"

Yancy shrugged agreement. "There's too much truth in what he says," he summed up. "The point is, he didn't have to say it."

"The guy's a troublemaker," Clint said, calming down a bit. "The Vulcans are still drawing big crowds, so they're not losing any money, which would hurt them most."

"Maybe that'll make 'em forget they're losing face," said Yancy hopefully.

"Don't count on it. I'm probably a born pessimist, but that's the way it is."

Clint's gloomy outlook was reduced a trifle by a bright ray that even pessimism could not dull. Even though he tried not to overemphasize his achievement, he could not deny the fact that he was learning to play football. The latent talent he possessed was swiftly coming to the surface, forcing him to recognize the true potential. He felt at times as if he must be dreaming, yet the dream persisted on the gridiron. He was playing the brand of football he had always hoped to play but had never dreamed was possible.

He was handling the ball with the assurance of a magician. His passing accuracy improved daily. He was reaching the stage where football instinct cooperated with his judgment—a big boost to the confidence he was able to impart to the other members of the team.

Yancy, too, was going through the same exciting transformation. He was developing the uncanny knack of being in the right spot at the right time. As a pass receiver he could outmaneuver the defense and catch the hard ones. As a defensive end he was becoming formidable.

"What's going on?" Clint asked Shag. "Will Yancy and I wake up some morning and find we've both been dreaming?"

"It's no dream," Shag assured him. "Football has been in you all the time and now it's starting to ooze out. You and Yancy are naturals. You've both got it."

"I hope we can keep it up. I hope we can win our last two games."

"It ought to be a breeze . . . unless—" he checked himself abruptly, frowning with the annoyance of a man who has said more than he intended to.

Clint waited a moment before saying, "Well?"

"Forget it. It's just a crazy hunch."

"But what's the hunch?" insisted Clint.

"No deal. I don't intend to sound off on something that may never happen. If it does happen, you'll know well enough what the hunch was all about."

Shag's hunch scored a bull's eye, rocking Clint with the unexpectedness of an earthquake. He could understand, when the hunch came true, why Shag had clammed up. He had not wanted to plant fantastic improbable ideas in the mind of his star quarterback.

Clint and Yancy were both in Clint's room one evening when they received a visitor, a big, muscular man in his middle thirties, with rusty hair. He entered the open door, and when he moved toward them, unannounced, with the air of a man who had a right to be there, his bearing conveyed both power and grace.

"I was hoping to find the two of you together," he said, by way of greeting.

Clint and Yancy weathered the first shock in exactly the same way. They were both frozen with astonishment. The ghost of Julius Caesar could not have handed them a greater jolt. They stared unbelievingly at their surprising guest—Barney Stack, head coach of the Vulcans.

Stack had to keep on carrying the ball. The other two were speechless. "I've come to ask a favor," he informed them, with the assurance of a man who knew the favor would be granted promptly.

"Of—of *us?*" demanded Clint incredulously.

Stack nodded. "I want you to report for the varsity. I need you."

The words had a strange effect on Clint. After the first tremor of disbelief his thoughts began to fall into their proper slots, making sense. He had little time to marvel at the fact that he was not grateful for Stack's offer.

He was even more amazed when a growing sense of outrage forced words out of him which he had no time to censor. "Just like that, huh?" he said harshly. "So now we're supposed to join your crew, because you need us? We tried to do that once before, mister. We signed up for football. We got pushed around, but good, then finally got swept out like a pile of dirt. We organized our own team. We made it click. And now, with two games left, you want us to run out on our own teammates like a pair of rats. Maybe you ought to have your head examined."

Barney Stack, exalted head coach of the Vulcans,

was not accustomed to be told off by a football player, not even by those he could not get along without. It showed in his expression—the quick involuntary frown of a man whose vast authority was doubted. He made a successful effort at self-control, which Clint had to chalk up to his credit.

"You've got a gripe," he told Clint gruffly. "I don't deny it. I'll admit, too, that our football system isn't perfect, and that, despite the fact that I'm only a hired hand, I have to accept some of the responsibility. I have to go along with the system or lose my job. It's as simple as that. I've got my problems, too, and one of them is to win football games."

"Maybe I went off half-cocked," Clint admitted grudgingly.

"We all do now and then," said Stack. "I wasn't kidding when I said I needed you and Yancy. Injuries and ineligibilities have hit us hard. We're hurting at the ends and in the quarterback department. Bronco Slade's back with us at quarterback, but frankly we can't depend on him, because of his swelled head and his temper. It looks," he added ruefully, "as if I jumped in on your boys a little too fast. I understand the way you feel, but I wish you'd think it over before you come to a decision. How about it?"

"We'll think it over," promised Clint.

When Stack had left, Yancy said, "Why think it

over? The situation is too perfect. We've got the jerks over a barrel, so let's leave 'em there."

Clint's impulsive burst of indignation was beginning to wear off, to be replaced by half-formed thoughts. Hazy though they were at this stage, he began to feel they were worthy of closer scrutiny.

"I'm not so sure," he said at last. "Maybe we *should* take a little time to think it over. There's something trying to get through to me, and I can't quite nail it down."

"I've got a funny feeling too," said Yancy. "Let's get a few more brains on the job. It's pretty big."

"I'll call Roger Grant."

The resulting conference was brief. Maggie Parnell and Grady Bell were also asked to come.

It was Maggie who came up with the clincher. "It boils down to this," she said. "Clint and Yancy could pay off a real grudge by refusing to join the Vulcans. On the other hand, your kids have worked mighty hard to establish the Rebels, and it certainly wouldn't hurt your cause to do the Vulcans a favor at this time. Does that make sense?"

The others nodded.

"There's more to it than that," continued Maggie. "What if Clint and Yancy made a good showing with the Vulcans? Just think it over. Wouldn't it mean that a team like the Rebels was a valuable asset to Midwestern; that the varsity, through no effort of its own, could find an occasional good man for its own use? How about it, Clint?"

Clint nodded thoughtfully, excitement rising gradually within him. "Yes," he said. "I like the sound of it. If Yancy and I could put on a good show, you Athletic Department folks would have to think twice before junking the Rebels."

"We really would," Maggie agreed.

A sudden thought dimmed Clint's enthusiasm. Maggie caught the change in his expression. "Now what?" she demanded.

"It's not my decision—or Yancy's. It's up to the other fellows on the squad. The Rebels have a good chance to win their last two games, and without being too swell-headed about it, I think they'll need Yancy and me to win them. They don't owe any more loyalty to the Vulcans than we do, and I don't see how we can run out on them at this time."

The stubbornness of his tone was not lost on the others. After a short silence Maggie said, "I think we'll all have to go along with that. Will you talk it over with them this afternoon?"

When Clint presented the proposition to the Rebels he received a prompt response—so prompt, indeed, that his suspicions were aroused. The situation had the earmarks of a kindly frame-up, as if the matter had been carefully explained beforehand to the Rebels. It was something Clint assumed but did not question. He had sense enough to accept things as they were.

Acting as spokesman, Archer said, "We'd all be fools to be stubborn about it. We've got to consider our team as a long-range project, and I think that Clint and Yancy could do us more good right now by going with the Vulcans than they could by staying with the Rebels. Sure, we'd hate to lose our last two games, but if we do, the big brass will have to do a lot of fast explaining to our fans, and that, in itself, ought to strengthen our position. What do the rest of you guys think about it?"

The Rebels lost no time in backing Archer's statement. They even managed, to their credit, to show a degree of enthusiasm. Clint was grateful to them all for making things so easy for him, because, when the moment came, he found it hard to leave. He knew, with an emotion which caused him no shame, that he was leaving something very valuable behind him—a part of his life, a priceless interval which could never be relived.

"Nuts!" said Yancy, as they headed for the storeroom to check out varsity uniforms. "My pappy's little boy feels just like bawlin'."

"Don't tempt me," Clint said, swallowing a lump. "I hope we're doing the right thing."

"I hope so too," said Yancy fervently.

CHAPTER
19

The Vulcan uniform felt strange on Clint. Its newness emphasized the newness of his venture, his approach to a strange world, where many pitfalls surely were awaiting him. Doubts scrambled through his mind. Could he prove that he was varsity material, that the Rebels had made an important contribution to the school?

He found it difficult, at first, to fit himself into the Vulcan pattern. The workouts, impersonal and efficient, were far removed from the casual, close-knit workouts of the Rebels. The elaborate locker room and the fine equipment of the training room filled him with no satisfaction. He missed the stuffy, crowded quarters of the Rebels.

He had not been quite sure what to expect from

the men themselves—resentment, probably, or at best, an amused attitude of superiority. It surprised him to find neither. They were just like other football players, friendly enough when time permitted. But the element of time, Clint soon found out, was the controlling factor of the squad.

Time, time, time. There never seemed to be enough of it. To waste a precious second of the work-out was a blot upon the record of the harried coaches. Efficiency, factory style, a production line in which each motion had to be accounted for was the watchword.

Clint, as a result, had little time for personal reflection. Pounced on by the coaches, he was rushed into production like a piece of raw material. They found flaws in him that he never knew existed. They molded him and polished him, preparing him for a moment when he might be needed—if the moment ever came.

That part of it worried Clint. He accepted the molding process as essential. He even enjoyed the job of mastering the more refined techniques of football. The disturbing question was: would he ever get a chance to use them? Could he ever put them into practice? No matter how he looked at it he was still in the role of a third-string sub.

No one bothered to answer the question for him, and the question, in the days that followed, did not answer itself. The coaches worked upon him hard, as if he was important, yet no one assured him that it was so.

Yancy was going through the same process. "We're just spare parts," he complained. "They want to be sure we're in good shape in case they want to use us. And if they never get around to using us, we might as well have stayed with the Rebels. We can't do them any good up here if they keep us on the bench."

"Maybe they'll put us in the Hampton game," Clint said hopefully.

"And maybe not," said Yancy, still disgruntled.

The Vulcans were training all their big guns on the final game of the season against the Stafford University Buckskins. It was one of those long-standing rivalries with everything at stake each year, a game in which a mediocre season could be more or less redeemed and a coach could salvage lots of tottering prestige.

The build-up was already under way, placards screaming, "Skin the Buckskins!" and all the other demonstrations calculated to arouse hysteria, and to make the Vulcan rooters believe that their team had a chance against the undefeated Buckskins.

The game played the previous week against the Hampton College Rams was a calculated breather. The scheduling committee had to hide embarrassed blushes when such a game showed on the list. The Rams, of course, would happily take their licking, then collect their share of the gate receipts, an important item in their skinny budget.

The game, once under way, developed as expected. The Rams had nothing with which to combat the Vulcans. Bronco Slade, now first-string quarterback, played the first few minutes of the game. When the score began to mount, Rick Storm went in for Bronco. The coaches had also been working hard on Storm, a recruited player with a lot of promise which, at this stage, had not materialized to any great extent. He was good, though not exceptional, as had been hoped.

However, no great talent was required against the Rams. Clint learned this, to his regret, when Coach Stack sent him in as quarterback to start the final period of the game. Stack, moved by remorse or sheer embarrassment, packed the Vulcan line-up with other lowly bench men, including Yancy.

Clint soon found out that his quarterbacking skill, if any, was completely wasted. Any play he called could gain ground without much opposition; certainly it was no credit to a quarterback. He did his best, but soon lost interest in the game, like the other Vulcans.

"Big deal," griped Yancy, as he headed for the showers with Clint. "We sure convinced 'em that they can't get along without us."

"Yeah," agreed Clint gloomily. "Big deal."

There was nothing ahead of the Vulcans now except the big one, and the final preparation for this game was a revelation to Clint. The Vulcan machine went into high gear. The players became puppets manipulated by the coaching staff. The public was barred from the secret sessions.

Clint felt he should resent the fact that he was a mere cog in a machine, yet he found resentment ebbing in reluctant admiration of the efficiency around him. He could understand the logic in the process, this striving toward perfection; and the urge began to grow in him to be a part of something perfect. The cost was high, but the challenge made it worth the effort.

It was hard for Clint to know how well he was fitting into the machine. No one told him. He was merely told what he was supposed to do. He became aware, through his almost constant fog of weariness, that the coaches were working on Rick Storm with equal concentration, hammering at him, drilling him with the same ruthless thoroughness they were lavishing on Clint.

The emotional build-up for the game was concluded with an outdoor bonfire rally of the student body. There was lots of noise, and lots of oratory aimed at boosting hopes of victory among the fans. The Vulcans had no part in this. They were tucked in bed to rest for the labor still to come.

Clint joined the Vulcans in the varsity room before the game. It was his first experience with a team of this caliber that was facing a game of great importance. He was curious, half expecting to find a group of men so thoroughly drilled as cogs in a machine that even their emotions were controlled. It was a weird thought and soon dispelled. The Vulcans were drawn fine, jumpy as grasshoppers, no different from the Rebels. Clint was oddly surprised to learn that regimentation of the strictest sort could not transform these men into anything but a bunch of nervous kids about to face a common enemy.

Clint tried to absorb some of their tension but found it beyond his reach. He nursed a tension of his own, of course, but nothing he could share. He was an outsider here. Buckskin, to Clint, was merely a name, without enough significance to raise the hackles on his neck.

When they reached the field Clint joined the lesser Vulcans for the warm-up. The Buckskins were also warming up. Clint watched them with a purpose, trying to implant within himself some feeling which would make him want to tear them limb from limb. He drew a blank. He could find no reason to dislike the guys.

He found his dislike centering, instead, upon a point that could do him no good whatsoever. His eyes fastened upon Bronco Slade, who postured and strutted on the field as if convinced that the eighty thousand fans were watching him alone. His attitude said, "Relax, folks. Bronco's here. How can the Vulcans lose with me at the controls?"

When the game got under way, Clint learned, with some resentment, that Bronco's self-esteem was perhaps well justified. The Vulcans won the toss and elected to receive. The kick came down the middle. Bronco hauled it in, making shrewd use of his blockers as he headed up the field. When the blocking petered out, he resorted to his power, bulldozing his way to the thirty-six-yard line, a formidable runback.

The fans loved it. The Vulcans liked it too, which could be seen in their snappy explosion from the huddle to the line of scrimmage. The play broke fast, a double fake, with the fullback charging the light side of an unbalanced line and the halfback faking a plunge into the heavy side. It required some fancy ball handling on the part of Bronco, but he pulled it off successfully, keeping the ball himself and slashing into the Buckskin backfield for a six-yard gain.

Bronco kept the march alive, mixing his plays

well, using himself as a decoy to keep the defense off balance. His passing, too, was accurate, his receivers capable. The drive continued, displaying beautiful precision, the ultimate result of intensive coaching. Bronco himself made the touchdown, faking a short pass, then running a keeper across the goal line behind perfect blocking. Bronco faked another run, then flipped a pass into the end zone for two extra points.

It was a brand of football Clint had never seen before. The sheer beauty of it made his heart beat faster. His excitement was still high, when an odd conviction worked its way into his mind. He gave it close attention, permitting this conviction to take form, to demonstrate its logic. Though willing to admit he was no authority on football, Clint knew he had witnessed a series of virtually perfect football plays— almost too perfect to make sense.

He began to reconstruct the plays, giving himself time to figure all the angles. The pattern gradually took form, making it easier for him to believe the thing he had just seen. He was able to recall that the Vulcan line had charged with the ferocity of aroused men. They had played with an explosive violence which was almost artificial, a violence which could easily have been generated by the knowledge that they were up against a better team—a team that had slapped down opponents who had licked the Vulcans.

Clint believed he had the answer now—an answer not too reassuring. The first surge of the Vulcans had been a product of their desperation. It was creditable and courageous, but how long, Clint wondered, could a team play football on that stimulus alone? Desperation was a perishable commodity, inevitably short-lived, because of the energy it devoured.

Clint turned his attention to Coach Stack, who was pacing up and down in front of the bench. Stack's face was serious and intent. He was not sharing the fans' joy. Clint speculated that the coach had reached the same conclusion he had reached—that the Vulcans' fuel was being squandered. Clint experienced no feeling of disloyalty in hoping that his theory would prove sound. It would offer satisfying proof of his ability to analyze a football situation. He owed nothing to the Vulcans.

The proof was a little slow in coming—but it came. The explosive playing of the Vulcans held up through the first period, during which they expended tons of energy. They kept their own goal line uncrossed, a fact that seemed to cause the Buckskins no concern. The visitors maintained the pressure with a sinister deliberation, quite as if they knew that time was on their side. They appeared to understand the Vulcans' plight, knowing their inspired play was bound to be short-lived. This was proved, to some extent, by the Vulcans' failure to sustain another touch-down drive.

The crumbling process started early in the second period. The Vulcans started off with a fine break when they recovered a fumbled punt on the Buckskin thirty-two-yard line. Bronco started the series with a fake reverse, then carried the ball himself for a try around the opposite end. The Buckskins, however, were keeping Bronco well covered now, and were not too badly fooled on this one. When they hauled him down at the line of scrimmage he cut loose with his first display of temper, slamming the ball back to the ground when he regained his feet. A few disapproving boos were let loose by the Vulcan fans.

Bronco faded for a pass on second down. One of the receivers had wormed his way into an open spot, but Bronco never had a chance to get the pass away. A Buckskin lineman powered his way into the Vulcan backfield to nail Bronco for a five-yard loss.

In the first place, the Buckskin player should not have been permitted through the line. The Vulcan left guard was at fault. In the second place, the invader should have been stopped, or at least slowed down, by the secondary pass protection. It was one of those bad breaks, however, that can happen to the best of teams.

Bronco failed to see it that way. He blew a gasket, picking the wrong time and place to do it. Bronco's words could not be heard from Clint's spot on the bench, but his attitude and gestures made the situation clear as he lashed out at his ineffective teammates. It was also clear that the Vulcans, as a team, resented the explosion.

Clint, inexperienced as he was in football, recognized the blunder. A quarterback, he knew, accepts psychological as well as technical responsibility. He must tune himself to the emotions of his squad. There are times to crack down on the players and times to bring them back into the groove by other methods. The Vulcans, Clint was certain, were in no mood now to listen to a tirade from their quarterback.

Once more his analysis appeared to be correct. Another pass play failed, fouled up by poor coordination. The Vulcans, annoyed now with their quarterback instead of themselves or the Buckskins, looked sloppy on the play. There was a question in Clint's mind as to whether Bronco Slade could snap them out of it.

The question grew as play resumed. A punt missed the coffin corner and went into the end zone, permitting the Buckskins to put it in play on their twenty-yard line. They began to move, steadily, relentlessly, as if this was the moment they had waited for. They punctured the Vulcans' faltering defense, indifferent to the replacements Stack sent in to stem the

tide. They scored a touchdown plus a two-point conversion, to tie the score, 8-8. They rolled to another
touchdown before the period ended. This time they
kicked the extra point, and took the lead at 15-8.

CHAPTER
20

The session in the dressing room between halves was a stormy one. Stack rode the Vulcans hard, individually and collectively. While still under a good head of steam, he cut loose on Bronco Slade, hurling words that drained the color out of Bronco's face.

Clint listened with a puzzled, almost shocked amazement. He could not doubt that Stack was hounding Bronco for a purpose. It seemed as if the coach was probing for the snapping point of Bronco's unpredictable anger, preferring to have it break here in the dressing room rather than upon the field. Bronco took it all, hot-eyed and sullen. He refused to crack.

Stack's effort generated a delayed reaction. The Vulcans got another big break on the opening play.

The Buckskin quarterback, Sid Keefer, took the kickoff on his five-yard line. A savage tackle was responsible for a fumble, recovered by the Vulcans on the twenty-one-yard line. The Vulcan fans came howling back to life, screaming for a touchdown.

They almost got one. Bronco went for it on the first play. He faded behind good protection, picked his end-zone spot, and whipped the ball with nice precision to the point his racing end would reach just as the ball arrived.

A Buckskin pass defender analyzed the play a shade too late for a possible interception. There was a chance, however, for him to get across in time to knock it down—a slim chance, and he made the most of it. He went into the air with a final desperate leap.

The ball and the Buckskin arrived at the same time. The Vulcan end, though he got his fingers on the ball, could not clamp down on it. The collision sent both men to the ground to join the ball. The umpire, covering the play, promptly signaled an incompleted pass.

It was a tough decision, one of those close ones that conceivably could have gone either way. From Clint's spot on the bench it looked as if the umpire could just as easily have called defensive pass interference, which would have meant a first down on the one-yard line for the Vulcans. It was a rough break for the Vulcans, and hard to accept calmly.

Bronco did not accept it calmly. Convinced that the umpire had robbed him of a possible touchdown, his temper exploded into fragments. He charged toward the umpire, shouting his displeasure in language unfit to print. The umpire promptly thumbed him from the game, and Bronco promptly knocked the umpire down with a wallop to the jaw.

The fans emerged from a moment of shocked silence to boo Bronco wholeheartedly as he was dragged forcibly from the field. Coach Stack, stormy-eyed, ignored Bronco in the press of more vital business. Rick Storm was already on his feet, ready to rush into the game.

Stack regarded him for an uncertain instant before making a swift decision. "Sorry, Rick," he said. "Clint! Come here!"

Clint, staring at Stack openmouthed, remained frozen to the bench.

"Move!" Stack roared at him.

Clint moved as if the bench had scorched him.

"You too, Yancy!" ordered Stack.

Yancy, grinning, joined the coach and Clint.

Stack turned to Clint. "Get that stupid look off your face. I've had my eye on you, whether you knew it or not. You wouldn't be going in there now unless

I'd figured you the best man for the job. Can you handle it?"

Clint, recovered from his first surprise, said, "Yes, I can handle it. Any orders?"

"Yes. Repeat the same play that just got fouled up, P-42. Now get in there!"

Clint and Yancy jogged on the field together, buckling their head gear. Neither spoke. Both had their individual problems at the moment. Clint's thoughts were racing, jostling one another. Weathering a brief surge of panic, he forced them to focus on one clear fact—his chance had come to help the Rebels. The thing that he had labored for was moving toward its climax. In the minutes just ahead he would have a chance to prove whether or not the Rebel project was a worthy cause. It was up to him and Yancy.

He faced another critical moment when he reached the Vulcans. They were watching him intently, uncertainty and doubt in their eyes. Their knowledge of this man who was here to run their team was sparse. To the Vulcans, Clint was still a student. To them it was incredible that Coach Stack should place a man like this in such a vital spot at such a vital time.

If Clint had considered all these things, his first impression of the Vulcans might have been very different. He was thinking only of the job ahead of him, and as a result these men filled him with no awe. It was not a pose. Clint regarded them as implements to further his own aim, men who had no part in his own life except as tools.

His attitude toward them, impersonal and barely civil, had a sharp effect. The uncertainty in the Vulcans' eyes began to fade. There was no meekness in Clint's manner, no apologetic aspect implying, "I'm not as good as you guys are accustomed to, but I'll do my best if you'll just give me a chance." On the contrary, his manner said, "Now we'll see just how good *you* guys are." The Vulcans might possibly have felt resentment, but resentment in this form was a tonic.

Clint, still concerned with the future of the Rebels, was unaware of what was taking place. He did know, however, that if he and Yancy were to make a worthy showing they would have to have a lot of help, and that such help would be easier to get if these men could be convinced that he and Yancy could really play football.

The opening play, Clint believed, would therefore be tremendously important. If it clicked, the process of gaining the Vulcans' confidence would receive a big boost in the right direction. It was illogical, Clint knew, to place so much importance on a single play, but that was the way he felt about it.

When he gave the signal in the huddle he experienced his first flash of uncertainty. His palms began to sweat. That was no good—not for a pass play. He dared not make the telltale gesture of drying them on his own uniform, so he wiped them surreptitiously on the broad rear of his center, as the big man crouched above the ball.

When the ball was snapped, Clint faded toward the side line, keeping as close as he dared to the line of scrimmage in case he had to turn the play into a keeper. He got good protection, permitting him to take brief advantage of the one thing in his favor—he was a stranger to the Buckskins and so was Yancy. The Buckskins had no way of knowing what to expect from the two replacements.

Clint focused his attention on the right side of the end zone, putting on as good an act as possible. Yancy, meanwhile, was staging his own act, loafing down the right side line as if he had no interest in the play. Rebel opponents had usually fallen for this one, at least once, and Clint gambled that the Buckskins were no different.

A Buckskin secondary man came through at Clint, who managed to avoid the tackle by a long twisting jump. He came down braced for the throw. Yancy, meanwhile, had uncorked an unexpected burst of speed, which took him behind the pass defender. Clint picked his end-zone spot, then whipped the pigskin flat and hard. It rifled just above the finger tips of several leaping Buckskins and reached its target in the end zone—Yancy. He pulled it in, head high. This time the umpire had no tricky choice to make. It was a touchdown all the way.

The fans went wild, but Clint, at this moment, was not concerned with happy fans. He was concerned entirely with the Vulcans, who, after their first stunned surprise, began to stare at him as if he were a man from outer space.

A few of them gave way to their emotion, acting natural and smacking Clint gratefully on the back. Clint, though he liked the feel of it, had sense enough to keep his own emotions bottled up. He had been lucky, and he was smart enough to know it. He had gained an important toehold with the Vulcans, and the way to keep it, he decided, was to maintain the attitude he had established at the start. He was still too much of an outsider to resort to familiarity with these men. It was a situation where a deadpan expression came in handy. Let them guess what he was thinking, if they could. In the meanwhile, let them all assume that he had come out here to boss the team and that he knew he had the stuff to do it.

Word came in from the bench to try a placekick for the extra point, a decision that made sense to Clint. Herb Finster, the fullback, was a fine place kicker at a short distance. If the kick was successful, the score would be tied 15-15. If the Vulcans took the greater risk of a two-point conversion and failed to pull it off, they would trail 15-14, and Clint agreed with Stack that it was not worth the risk. A tie score at this stage of the game would keep the Vulcans under considerably less pressure than the disturbing knowledge that they were trailing in the game. It would give them a better chance to adjust themselves to their new quarterback.

This adjustment, as Clint knew, was vitally important. It was one of those intangible factors that could make the difference between a win or a loss. If the men developed confidence in Clint, it would be a great aid to Clint as well as to the Vulcans. He had made a step in the right direction. The trick now was to keep them believing that he knew his job.

Finster made the kick, and on the next play the Buckskins ran the Vulcan kickoff back to the twenty-two-yard line, a so-so return that Clint chose to believe significant. The Vulcans had come down fast under the ball and had battered through the Buckskin defense with the air of men who had found something new to fight for.

There was a difference in the Buckskins, too. The sudden change of score had aroused them to the fact that they still had quite a job ahead of them. They settled down to it with efficient grimness. They began to move, grinding out the yardage on the ground, and three first downs carried them into Vulcan territory on the forty-yard line. The Vulcan fans pleaded loudly for their boys to stop the march, pleas that seemed to be effective.

The Vulcan defense stiffened. A line play was held to a three-yard gain. The Buckskins tried a reverse around the Vulcan right end. Clint waited in his deep spot until he saw a Buckskin lineman reach the Vulcan backfield. Knowing, then, that there was no chance of a forward pass, Clint came in fast.

Yancy, meanwhile, had refused to be blocked out of the play, or rather, partially out of it. He slid off a sideswipe from a Buckskin player, retaining his balance long enough to make a long dive at the runner. Yancy got a hand on the man's jersey, gripping it long enough to swing the Buckskin half around before he tore away. Clint, arriving just about then, slashed in with a low tackle, slamming the runner to the ground before the man could gain traction on the turf. The play went for a scant two yards.

With third down and five to go, the Buckskins took to the air. Sid Keefer, their quarterback, was a first-rate pass or run man, but when Clint saw that no Buckskin linemen were invading the Vulcan backfield, he paid full attention to the Buckskin right end, who was cutting down the side line.

Clint noted, as he moved toward the danger zone,

that the end was almost *too* close to the side line, which
meant that any pass tossed to that spot would run the
risk of being caught out-of-bounds. It must be supposed, therefore, that the end intended to cut in toward
the center of the field.

He did just that, and Clint was ready for him.
Refusing to overrun his man, Clint was poised to
swerve when the Buckskin player swerved. Clint's reasoning paid off. When the end cut swiftly in, Clint had
him covered like a tent. Watching the end's eyes, Clint
knew the ball was in the air. He whirled, timing his
jump precisely as he saw the pigskin flashing toward
him. He let his hands fade with the ball, reducing the
shock of contact. He had the ball locked safely in his
arms when the outraged Buckskin hurled him to the
ground.

The Vulcan fans went crazy. Some of the Vulcans
lost their reserve again and slapped congratulations on
Clint's back. It was a little harder, this time, for Clint to
retain his own reserve. He resented the effort it cost
him, until he reminded himself that he was not in here
to help these guys, but to help the Rebels.

The interception helped to boost Clint's stock a
little higher, which was all to the good. He even began
to worry a little for fear that he might not be able to
justify the good opinions of his teammates and the

spectators, as the game went on. He banished this worry as well as he could, determined to concentrate on the job at hand.

Toward this end he worked a series of handoffs from a tight-T. The Vulcans, driving hard, squeezed out a first down on the forty-six-yard line, and during that series of close plays, Clint learned more than blackboard diagrams could ever have taught him.

The knowledge was both exciting and stimulating. It was as if he had been playing until now with toy machinery, as if only at this moment had he experienced the real thing, the polished mechanism that responded to a touch. It was a thrill he had never known before, and he was honest enough to admit it to himself.

Even in this brief period, he was aware of the effects his new skill had upon him. Not only did it increase his enjoyment of the game, it was producing facets of his own game he had never before been aware of. His ball handling became swifter and more assured, because he knew that all the parts of his complicated machine were trustworthy. He also had the notion that the feeling was mutual, that he was imparting confidence and sureness to the other Vulcan players. He could afford to concentrate more closely now upon the other team, assured that the men behind him and in front of him all knew their jobs.

Unfortunately, the Buckskins also knew theirs. Their confidence was as great as, if not greater than, the Vulcans', a condition they promptly settled down to prove. The Buckskins, too, were geared high and precisely tuned.

The Vulcans got a bad break on the opening play of the next series, yet Clint was inclined to believe that the break, in the long run, might prove more beneficial than harmful. It happened when he faded for a pass. A Buckskin lineman came catapulting into the Vulcan backfield, nailing Clint for a five-yard loss.

Rising from the ground, Clint told his men, "I should have been able to side-step *that* big ape."

Art Machen, the big guard who had let the Buckskin through the line, stared hard at Clint. "Are you kidding?" he demanded. "You know right well I should have stopped him."

Clint grinned. "I should have dodged him, too," he said.

He saw a strange thing happen to the Vulcans, swift but unmistakable. The silent glances they exchanged told Clint they were comparing him to Bronco Slade. Bronco would have blown his top, creating tension. Clint, blaming no one, had calmly accepted the fact that such things were bound to happen. It was another long step in the right direction, another nail to fasten down the confidence these men were developing in Clint.

Clint played a hunch on the next play, calling a thoroughly illogical signal for this kind of situation. In the huddle, he said to Art Machen, "Can you open a hole for me?"

Machen shot him a surprised look, then said grimly, "Try me."

"O.K., it's a sneak."

If Clint surprised his own teammates on the choice of plays, he surprised the Buckskins even more. They were obviously unprepared for a quarterback stupid enough to call a sneak on second down with fifteen yards to go.

Art Machen exploded into the Buckskin line like an enraged gorilla. The center, Joe Gratz, teamed up with him. The tackle on that side of the line slid into the Buckskin backfield by permitting his opposing tackle to charge harmlessly into the Vulcan backfield.

Clint, meanwhile, was following Art Machen like a jeep following a tank. Once across the line Clint had a brief instant to take advantage of the Buckskins' astonishment. He made the most of it. He shoved clear of Machen, following his tackle toward the side line. The tackle threw a key block. Clint reached the side line, where he did a tightrope act until the deep defense man got across to blast him out-of-bounds.

It was a fourteen-yard gain. Clint sent his fullback, Finster, on a straight line back to pick up the extra yard, and for a stomach-shriveling interval, it looked as if Finster had not made it. The chain came in. It was close, too close. Clint breathed again when the referee made a welcome sweeping gesture toward the Buckskin goal line. First down.

The Buckskins, however, came to life and slammed the door. They were peeved, alert, and smart. Having already spotted Clint and Yancy as a major passing threat, they readjusted their defense to hold the threat to a minimum.

In this they were successful as the game went on. Clint completed his share of passes—probably more than his share, under the circumstances—but none of the completed passes endangered the Buckskin goal line.

The Buckskins got their big break in the early minutes of the final period. With the ball on the Vulcan forty-three-yard line, the Buckskins broke Sid Keefer into the clear for a long run. Clint managed to bounce him out-of-bounds on the fourteen-yard line, but the Vulcans were now in a very dangerous spot. They responded valiantly, holding for three downs. The Buckskins tried a field goal on fourth down, and made it good. The score was 18-15.

A wave of gloom rolled toward the field from the Vulcan fans. Clint waited for it to engulf the Vulcans. He waited curiously, almost impersonally, wondering if the wave would sweep them under, wondering how these men, still strangers to him, would withstand it.

A feeling of amazement, mixed strongly with confusion, came slowly over him. The wave had scarcely touched them—only briefly, if at all. In a moment of unexpected clarity he was actually seeing the Vulcans for the first time. These men refused to be discouraged, despite the odds against them.

It showed more clearly as the play continued. Clint had to believe that a crisis of this sort was designed to separate the men from the boys, to bring out qualities in men that do not appear upon the surface. He was watching these qualities appear now—doggedness and determination, bolstered by a great desire to win.

The transformation within Clint himself was slow but very sure. It changed his outlook on the game, his outlook on himself. To this point, he had been playing entirely for the Rebels. He had not considered it a selfish goal. He did not consider it so now. He only knew that something new and rather powerful had been added.

He had placed the Vulcans in the indifferent category of paid performers. His mistake was obvious. These men were football players, playing, just as he played, for their great love of the sport. Whether they were subsidized or not, their emotions were essentially the same as his own. They were playing for the sport itself, not for the money or even for the education it provided.

Clint would have been aware of his mistake much earlier if his own thoughts had not been occupied with what he had hoped to accomplish for the Rebels. Well, he had accomplished it—if that was possible. Both he and Yancy had contributed the proof that they were varsity material.

It now remained for Clint to put his new knowledge to the test. He found it easy. Win or lose, his enjoyment of the game was increasing in these final minutes. These men were now *his* men. He felt close to them, a change they may have recognized unconsciously, a closer unity, a subtle stimulus.

At any rate, they managed to unearth some hidden force that helped them mount a strong offensive as the seconds ticked away. They played like maniacs, without sacrificing their coordination. Clint led them with a new, effective understanding. Time, however, was now their relentless enemy—an enemy that promised to destroy them.

They reached the twenty-eight-yard line, third down, two yards to go, with fifteen seconds left to play. Clint had already called time out, awaiting instructions from the bench. The Vulcans had no kicker with much chance to tie the score at that long distance from the goal posts. Stack's instructions came—a pass. What else?

Clint gave the signal in the huddle. "They'll be expecting it," he added. "If they have the receivers too well covered I may have to run with it. Keep that in mind and keep your eyes on me. It's our last chance and I may need a lot of help."

The Buckskins were, of course, expecting Clint to pass. Their defense was spread for the emergency— shrewdly spread to indicate that they, too, were considering the possibility of a running play if Clint could find no one to pass to.

Clint took the snap from center, fitting the ball snugly to his hand as he faded toward the side line. His forward wall held solidly, giving Clint all the time he needed, time enough to tighten his throat and make his stomach crawl at the efficiency of the Buckskin pass defense. All possible receivers were completely covered.

Clint had more or less expected it to be this way. He snatched a deep lungful of breath and drove his legs into motion, running with a controlled speed that permitted blockers to get out ahead of him.

The Buckskins, too, had more or less expected Clint to run. The thing the visitors had not prepared for was the savage, last-ditch violence of the Vulcans, who exploded every ounce of energy left in them.

They hacked a path for Clint, a small and crooked one. Clint wormed through tiny openings, too occupied with other things to wonder how he did so. He only realized that he had never made a dizzy, twisting run like this before with equal perfection. All the football instinct he possessed, together with a lot he never knew he had, was concentrated in this final effort. He had the weird sensation that an unseen hand was guiding him.

A Buckskin player hit him from behind while the goal line was still several strides away. The tackle, fortunately, was high. Clint staggered from the impact. His legs began to buckle. He forced them to stay under him until a final violent lunge sent him to earth. His eyes were closed. He was afraid to open them. When he finally forced himself to do so, he could see the white stripe of the goal line underneath the ball.

The Vulcans, yelling like a bunch of crazy men, hauled Clint to his feet and mauled him. It was the sort of mauling Clint could take a lot of in his present frame of mind. The Vulcans missed the extra point, but who cared? The kickoff in the five remaining seconds was a mere formality. There was no long runback, and the game was over.

There was a wild celebration in the Vulcan dressing room. When things had quieted a bit, Roger Grant drew Clint aside. There was a smug expression on

Grant's face. "I've got news for you," he said, "with the compliments of Mr. Herbert Crawford. He felt that I had the right to tell you first, though he'll be here soon to confirm it."

"Your expression says it's good news," Clint guessed, feeling weak inside.

"The best. The Rebels, from here in, will be a part of the athletic program. How does that strike you?"

"Don't ask foolish questions."

"O.K., I won't. Here comes Herb Crawford. He's really a good guy, and I think you'll like him."

"I'm prepared to—now," said Clint.